OPERATOR 5:
THE ARMY OF THE DEAD

SECRET SERVICE OPERATOR #5 ™
AMERICA'S UNDERCOVER ACE

THE ARMY
OF THE DEAD

By Curtis Steele

STEEGER BOOKS • 2020

PUBLISHING HISTORY

"The Army of the Dead" originally appeared in the March, 1935 (Vol. 3, No. 4) issue of *Operator #5* magazine. Copyright © 2020 by Argosy Communications, Inc. All rights reserved.

CHAPTER 1
PROCESSION OF CORPSES

HARD-PRESSED BRAKES suddenly slowed the streamlined roadster. Its tires whined and ground in loose grit. The treble song of its powerful Diesel engine dropped to a whisper. Its bright headlamps shafted past a raw bank of earth, into a pool of blackness lying directly ahead. It slid toward the brink of a cavity into which the road disappeared—a yawning hollow waiting to trap the unwary.

For long hours, the roadster had been racing over winding highways, shuttling deep into the bleak hills of this coal-mining district in Pennsylvania. Its headlights had probed across sheer-walled valleys, beyond high-crested slopes, seeking an isolated destination that lay far from the bustling cities of the Eastern seaboard. Hundreds of miles had spun beneath its wheels. Once out of New York City, once beyond the Hudson, it had sped with scarcely a stop—until now.

It skidded to a standstill in a black, silent world. No light glimmered in all this vast, rugged land save its headlamps. No sound disturbed the night save the muffled sighing of its motor. Its fuming brakes stilled its wheels just this side of the black maw into which the road dipped. Except for the swift, alert action of the driver, it would have plunged into the hollow; a crashing doom would have destroyed it and brought instant death to its passengers.

1

Along the street came the procession of the dead— Corpses borne on litters!

The young man at the wheel leaned forward to peer ahead intently. At the edge of the cavity, countless footprints marked the dust. A framework of beams lay like a giant skeleton in the depths. On the far side weather-worn planks, pierced by rusty spikes, were piled. Near them rose a gaunt signpost, pointing a direction it was now impossible to take, and its legend read mockingly:

Carbonville 3 Miles

"Three miles to the village," the driver said softly. "Three feet to eternity."

The dash-lights glowed on his cleanly chiseled face, in his gleaming blue eyes. He was young—in his early twenties. He was obviously American to the core. The slender fingers of his right hand were tightened around the wheel, and on the back of that hand shone a peculiar scar—a pattern of black and white and gray that formed, uncannily, the picture of a spread-winged American eagle. As he straightened, those supple fingers strayed unconsciously toward an ornament he wore on his watch-chain—a cunningly contrived golden charm, a death's head with eyes that glittered red fire.

His name was James Christopher. In the secret archives of the United States Intelligence Service, he was designated Operator 5.

Operator 5 threw the roadster into reverse abruptly. He turned it end for end, sent it speeding in the direction he had come. A fraction of a mile away, he swerved into a side road. The car rolled with scarcely a tremor over bumps that loomed like boulders in the shafts of the headlamps, descending a steep grade into a black-flooded valley, winding its way deeper into the isolation of the unsettled hills.

"Our destination," he declared calmly, "is still Carbonville."

His two companions studied his face. The boy perched alertly beside him was round-eyed, alert, troubled. Tim Donovan was in his teens; yet the courageous Irish lad had greatly assisted Operator 5 in cases of momentous importance. He wore a white-metal ring of strange design—a skull emblazoned on a black

4

background, its forehead marked by the mystic numeral 5. All United States Intelligence agents in the world had been informed that by this ring the boy could be recognized as the unofficial assistant of Operator 5.*

"Jimmy!" he exclaimed. "There weren't any red lanterns at that bridge—no warning signs. Somebody must've deliberately torn it up to keep traffic away from Carbonville."

"Right, old-timer," Jimmy Christopher answered quietly. "We're not welcome tonight—nor is anyone else coming from this direction. I intend to find out why."

THE MAN seated beside Tim Donovan blinked thoughtfully. He was round-faced, apparently a stolid and unthinking type; yet he was one of the keenest undercover agents in the United States Intelligence. He was known as X-11. He said curiously:

"You've certainly got me guessing, Operator 5. I know there's a big strike at the Wharton mines—but why should you be interested in labor troubles? I've also read the report that six miners are trapped in a cave-in in one of the shafts, but that can't be what's bringing you here tonight. Are you handling the

---

* AUTHOR'S NOTE: This ring was designed by Operator 5 and presented by him to Tim Donovan. The membership rings worn by the Secret Sentinels of America differ from it in only one slight particular. This detail, however, cannot be disclosed here.

case of Hamilton Wharton's disappearance? That's a bit out of your line, too. I suspect there's another reason."

"There is another reason," Jimmy Christopher admitted. "I'm following the strangest trail I've ever picked up. It's a weird hunch. If I told you why I've brought you here tonight, you'd think me mad. Without you as a witness, X-11, my report might seem like the wild imaginings of a—"

Again Operator 5's foot shot to the brakes and the wheels of the roadster crunched through grinding grit. The car lurched to a slower speed while Jimmy Christopher braced himself and peered through the windshield, into the shine of the headlights. He straightened and exclaimed, "Again!"

The three men in the car gazed in astonishment at a high mound of earth and rocks which reared in the road. It completely cut off the way—an obstruction unmarked by lanterns or warning signs. Just around a bend, threatening the unwary driver with a violent collision, loomed the heap of doom.

"Jimmy—look!" Tim Donovan gasped. "It's all been torn out of that bank. There's a shovel. Somebody deliberately put it there!"

"Right again, Tim!" Operator 5 answered between taut lips. His blue eyes took on a darker tone as he spoke. "If we followed a third road, I'm sure we'd find a third obstruction. It's reasonable to believe that every approach to Carbonville is barred tonight. I still intend to find out why."

He backed the car, swinging it so that its headlights swept across the rolling land. Abruptly he sent the roadster jouncing off the pavement onto a steep slope. The powerful motor throbbed as Operator 5 sought his way past the barrier. The car tilted at a dangerous angle; Tim Donovan and X-11 balanced themselves breathlessly. Jimmy Christopher made the roadster crawl past the looming mound, then he nosed it downward to the road again.

Once he turned it on the pavement, he pressed the accelerator and blinked off the lights. Tense at the wheel, he drove along a strip of black almost invisible in the night. Fog drifted through the low valley borne by a slow wind. Operator 5's eyes conned the distance; he listened through the smooth hum of the motor. There was no gleam, no other sound, no sign of the men who had barred the roads....

Then, suddenly, black figures leaped into the open field from the shelter of blacker bushes. They sprang out from both sides, gripping upraised cudgels, rushing toward the roadster. They appeared like ghosts; they came in a savage swarm. Instantly Jimmy Christopher's hand darted to the switch and the shafts of his headlights shot ahead.

Grimy faces shone in the glare—hard faces, eyes glittering with a fanatical light. The shadow figures became men garbed in blackened overalls; the hands that gripped the cudgels were sooty and huge. Men of brutal strength, driven by desperation, they crowded to block the road and surround Operator 5's car.

"Git back!"

"Clear out or by God we'll destroy yer!"

"Give it to 'em!"

Jimmy Christopher sensed a swift movement from X-11— who was reaching toward a gun. He warned: "Don't touch it!"

as he pressed the accelerator. The roadster leaped ahead under a sudden surge of power—straight toward the herding men! Grimly he spurted toward them, hands whitened on the wheel, blue eyes clouding dark.

A SAVAGE howl tore from the throats of the attackers as they leaped aside. They scrambled to escape the rush of Operator 5's roadster. He twisted the wheel frantically, weaving the car skillfully to avoid hitting any of them. As the darting figures blurred by, the car jarred under the power of swift blows. The guardians of the road crashed their cudgels on the fenders as Jimmy Christopher streaked through them.

He sent the car plunging at its limit of power—and again he clicked out the lights. Shrouding darkness returned to the road. Peering back, Tim Donovan glimpsed the black men running after the car, swinging their weapons, shouting in wrath. They disappeared into the gloom as Jimmy Christopher swung around an almost invisible bend and sent the car humming up a dangerous slope.

He flew across the crest of it and, as a panorama of rolling hills opened before him, he slowed. In that vast area of darkness, lights sparkled. Ahead, covered by a glowing aura, lay a village—Jimmy Christopher's destination, Carbonville. It was still a mere oasis of light in the spreading wilderness of the night when he swung abruptly off the pavement.

He sent the car jouncing across a rather rough slope; he twisted it into the thicker darkness hovering beneath a clump of trees. With brakes jammed hard, with the Diesel clicked off, he sat tensely listening. Not until he was satisfied that the sentries had been left far behind, that he had reached this hiding-place unseen, did he slip out.

He gazed into the glow in the hills and sensed an unseen activity. There was a flicker in the shine as of naked flames burning. Operator 5 watched silently as his slender fingers strayed unconsciously to his watch-chain.

Reports coming to secret Intelligence Headquarters B-3 in New York had informed him of the details of the strike that was disrupting the great coal-mines at Carbonville. The violence of the industrial warfare between the miners and the mine-owners had grown day by day. The first outbreak had occurred following a disastrous cave-in in a deep shaft—an accident that had imprisoned six men in the black depths of the earth. Operator 5 recalled the headline of the last news dispatch that had come out of these embattled hills:

MINERS TRAPPED WITHOUT AIR;
CERTAIN ALL SIX ARE DEAD!

The disappearance of Hamilton Wharton, chief owner of the coal-mines, following close on the heels of the disaster, had thrown the other officials of the great Wharton Corporation into a frenzy. He had vanished while en-route by automobile from his home in New York to the mine property. His empty car had been found a charred ruin beside the road near Carbonville. That he had been taken by the angered strikers was almost a certainty; yet no clue to his whereabouts had been found....

Here in this isolated town, a kettle of devil's-brew was boiling—yet Operator 5 was thinking now of the men who had

9

attacked him, of the ringing shouts that had carried threats on the night wind.

"They did not shout: 'We'll kill you!'" he observed in a voice so low it was almost a whisper. "They said, 'destroy—*destroy!*' "

OPERATOR 5 started down the steep, stubbled slope. Tim Donovan and X-11, alert and wondering, trailed him. They fought their way through jungle-thick bushes; they crept through boulder-strewn passes; when they paused, they were close to the edge of the town. Jimmy Christopher cautioned silence and warned:

"There must be other guards. We'll have to work carefully to get past them. Follow me, and take no chances!"

He worked his way alertly toward a block of buildings flanking a street that crossed the main thoroughfare. He gazed along it to see the sidewalks thronged. Hundreds of men in blackened coveralls, women with coats drawn snug against the biting night air, children clinging to the hands of their parents; they lined the curbs, silent and waiting. They peered toward a point outside the town, where the darkness flickered as with the light of naked flames.

Suddenly a chorus rose from the crowd—a rising voice of expectancy that issued from every throat, a muted song that bespoke both grief and hope. Every eye turned toward the distance as the tone rose with the throbbing depth of a mighty organ. And as it took on a rhythm, as it beat into a swelling chant, the flickering of the lights grew nearer and stronger.

"They come!" The shouts rang out.

"They come!"

"The dead are coming to live again!"

While the chant sent its rhythm echoing through the night, Jimmy Christopher moved silently closer to the buildings. With Tim Donovan and X-11 close at his side, he trod along a street  that was slowly losing its gloom. The flickering lights beyond grew stronger; the beat of marching feet came with the growing luminescence. Shadowed in a doorway, unseen by the crowds, Operator 5 peered down the lined street and saw many torches.

Torches, held aloft, bare flames whipping in the night wind, black smoke trailing into the black night, glittered their light into the gleaming faces of the chanting hundreds. They were held high in the hands of coveralled men striding in double file. Behind them other men marched, in units of four, and each team of four were carrying a litter. On the litters, men lay motionless—men whose upturned faces were contorted in expressions of horrible agony—men who were dead....

Along the street came the procession of the dead. Only their faces were visible—faces turned skyward, glazed eyes gazing blindly into the depths of the dark heavens, faces blackened by coal-dust and blanched with death. Yet the corpses on the litters lay beneath luxurious coverlets of crimson silk. A golden fringe twinkled on the edges of the shrouds, and in the center of the gleaming crimson was an emblem outlined in black—a royal crown!

The corpses passed by in ghastly parade, each shrouded in

crimson while the chanting of the hundreds beat upon their ears that could not hear. And there were six of them.

The crowd pressed thickest at the front of a church which once had been white. From it radiated a brilliant light. It stood outlined against the night—an infidel temple. Its windows did not shine with the colored mosaics of the Christian saints; each was an emblem of blood-red marked in black with the symbol of the royal crown. Its spire reared high above the chanting crowd, topped—not by a golden cross—but with a crown of gold! Toward the open portals of the Temple of the Crown the procession of corpses turned.

"They come!"

"They come!"

"The dead have come to live again!"

HIGHER IN pitch, fanatical in fervor, the song mounted as the last of the marching file appeared. Again four men, garbed as miners, tramped with inexorable rhythm; but these four were not carrying a litter between them. Their hands gripped chains. The chains were bound to the pinioned wrists, to the arms and the body of a fifth man held between them.

The prisoner was jerked along, step by step, as he strove desperately to escape the bonds of iron. He was garbed in a black business suit of costly tailoring; his hair was iron-gray; his face was strong, yet fear gleamed in his eyes—a fear that mounted visibly with the drumming rhythm of the chant. The yellow light of the torches gleamed brightly upon his bearded, whitened face.

From Operator 5's lips a name burst: "Hamilton Wharton!"

12

He drew back quickly. Hamilton Wharton, bound beyond the strength of any man, was dragged toward the doors of the crimson-windowed temple. At each step he struggled to tear away, but the chains pulled him on mercilessly. Behind him the crowd surged, mobbing into the temple; from within the walls the muted song continued to rise.

Jimmy Christopher signaled quickly when the crowd began to eddy into the side street He retraced his steps with Tim Donovan and X-11 at his sides. He paused in deep shadow, and they peered in wonderment into his darkened eyes.

"Those dead," he said quietly, "are the six who were trapped in the mine shaft. Their bodies have been recovered. They—"

"God!" X-11 exclaimed. "What are those men going to do with Wharton? They're dragging him along as though they intend to make him a sacrifice to some heathen idol! These people are mad!"

"Mad," Operator 5 answered quietly, "and crying out their fear of death."

He watched the crowd alertly. It had parted; it was now pouring into the temple also through a side entrance. Jimmy Christopher shifted to a spot from which he could see the rear of the converted church, and noted a door that was guarded. He drew X-11 close and Tim Donovan listened wide-eyed.

"We've got to get inside. We don't stand a chance dressed as we are. There's only one possible way—and we've got to take it. Once we're inside, we've got to try to get Wharton free of those men—if he is to be a sacrifice."

"Good God—do you actually believe that?" X-11 blurted. "Is

The blade in the hand
of the crowned figure
began to descend…!

it possible that civilized human beings, for any reason, would take the life…?"

"If the grip of death upon human beings has actually been broken," Jimmy Christopher interrupted quickly, "there is nothing that we may not believe possible."

He strode across the bleak street quickly. X-11 and Tim Donovan hurried after him into the shadow of an adjacent building. Sheltered by thick darkness, they listened to the continued chant of the hundreds crowding into the temple. There was a ringing note of fanaticism in the voice of the assembly—like a plaintive cry of hope. It struck deep into the mind of Operator 5 as he moved alertly to the rear of the temple.

He became a shadow that appeared suddenly near the two coveralled men at the door. X-11 materialized behind him as the pair whipped about. Tim Donovan glimpsed their hard faces, their desperate eyes, as they shouldered together to block the way. Their great hands reached out and one of them snarled:

"Hold on! You don't belong here!"

"Git back!"

A HUGE, hard fist slashed toward Operator 5's face. He sidestepped alertly; his answering blow was black lightning. His stiff fingers struck hard to the forehead of the man nearest him; they twisted deftly between the eyes. A sharp intake of breath sounded and the miner's body stiffened. He toppled like an unbalanced statue as Jimmy Christopher whirled to the second.

X-11's blow was blocked by a quick defense of the other miner. Operator 5 stepped swiftly to thrust the secret agent aside. Again he struck; again his stiff fingers drove home a skilled

16

jiu-jitsu blow. The instant response was an explosion of breath and a rigidity of the coveralled man's body. Operator 5 whirled, caught him as he tottered, and lowered him to the black ground.

He rose, listening. He knew that the blows would keep the two men unconscious for the better part of an hour. The fight had occurred with scarcely a sound. No alarm came from within the closed door.

"Quick!" Operator 5 ordered. "Strip them! Get into their clothes. Tim—watch!"

They dragged the two unconscious men deeper into the shadows. Tim Donovan stayed near the door, alertly watching the street. Soon he heard a rustle of movement behind him. He turned to see two men in miners' garb approach. Operator 5 and X-11 had rubbed their faces and hands with dirt and pulled their caps low. At the door, they listened to the continued chant within the temple.

"Stick close!" Jimmy Christopher warned. "Stay out of the light as much as possible. And be prepared for anything!"

The thunder of the hundreds of voices surged upon him as he opened the door. He slipped into a dimly lighted room, with X-11 following, with Tim Donovan at his side. From a point near the door, straight across the room, a heavy black curtain hung from floor to ceiling; behind it, there were sounds of movements. Jimmy Christopher felt eyes watching him, and passed on. He strode through the narrow space between the wall and the curtain; his manner proclaimed that he knew his way. He paused at another door; and again he stepped through.

It opened into the choir-stall. Beyond partly drawn curtains, the interior of the thronged temple was visible. Jimmy Christopher turned quickly toward an opening at his left, beside the old organ. He stepped into a gloomy musty space behind the pipes. Immediately he pressed close to them, and through the spaces he glimpsed the dais.

Gold glittered in the light—a golden crown lying on the pulpit. On the platform stood the torch-bearers, their eyes glinting in the shine. Six litters were placed in a row before them—six dead men lay beneath the coverlets of crimson satin, each marked with the sign of the crown. The hush of death was lost in the swelling chant of the multitude crowding into every inch of space within the temple.

"The dead will live!"

"Death takes us no more!"

"Hail the Master of Death!"

Suddenly the throbbing mass-voice was muted to a whisper. The song became a sigh of hopeful, fanatical reverence. The flames of the torches seemed to spring higher with a new life. Their gleams brightened upon the scarlet shrouds of the six who lay dead. The line of torch-bearers parted, drawing away from a crimson curtain that stretched behind the pulpit. The glistening folds stirred as if with a wind—a wind that could not be felt, but which bespoke a presence about to appear. And silence came....

Peering through the pipes of the old organ, Operator 5 saw the crimson curtains part. A figure stepped through. It was at first a mere outline in shining color—a being of crimson against a background of crimson. A tall man appeared, then, completely enwrapped in the color of blood. His robe covered his whole body. His head was enveloped in a cap of red silk. He stood motionless, peering at the silent assembly, his face hidden.

Slowly he advanced. With hands gloved in red, he reached toward the golden crown on the pulpit. It glittered in the light of the flames as he raised it. He placed it upon his head. From the lips of the hundreds, the voice burst again, crying out in fervent awe:

"Hail the Master of Death!"

CHAPTER 2
LIFE FOR THE DEAD

SILENCE—THICK SILENCE—FOLLOWING the cry, suffused the temple, and covered the corpses which lay on the dais. Silence, until the red crowned figure's muffled tones carried a command into die hush:

"*Yajna!*"

Chains clanked in answer. At the entrance of the temple there was movement. At the foot of the aisle, the four miners appeared gripping the chains which imprisoned the distraught, white-haired man. Every gaze in that strange assembly turned toward the captive as he was brought forward. Each step of the way he struggled, but he was tugged upon the steps, brought to the center of the rostrum. There he grew quiet; there his resistance faded as he peered at the figure cloaked in the color of blood.

Again the muffled voice carried into the hush of the temple as the robed man spoke to Hamilton Wharton. "The dead require your soul!"

He stood back. The four men dragged Wharton to the pulpit, and drew the chains tight, binding them around it, drawing the captive's head and shoulders back across the spot where the golden crown had sat. They hooked the links together and withdrew, leaving Wharton helpless. The crowned, red figure stepped forward again. His voice rumbled:

"Carry the dead into the chamber where life awaits them!"

Other men advanced to lift the litters bearing the corpses. The crimson curtain was drawn aside, disclosing a door. One by one, the bearers of the dead lifted their burdens. One by one, the corpses were carried through the crimson drapes, into the curtained space beyond. At one side, the Master of Death waited, gazing at the face of each passing cadaver. And as the last vanished into the secret space beyond, he turned with lifted red hands to the tense congregation:

"Raise your voices, my followers! Raise your voices to the dead who are about to live again!"

From the throats of the multitude the tones rose again, throbbing with the unholy chant. Consecrated walls vibrated with the power of that fanatical cry. As it swelled, the figure robed in crimson parted the curtains; as he passed through, the beating song assumed a frantic pitch. The light of the torches shone over the congregation—and upon the man chained helpless to the desecrated altar.

Coldly, Operator 5 leaned close to the dusty pipes of the organ, watching the fluttering red curtains. Behind it there was a sense of activity. Through it came strange sounds—a soft, rhythmic beating like the amplified throbbing of a living heart. Sibilant breaths issued from the draped space, as though a dying giant were struggling for breath. The torches flared; the chant of the congregation continued; behind the crimson curtains, men engaged in a task of mystery....

Jimmy Christopher turned at a touch on his arm. X-11 was leaning close, his face pale beneath its smear of grime, his eyes widened with a terror of the unknown. "In God's name, what is happening here?" he breathed. "They're all speaking of bringing the dead back to life! They're mad, every one of them! We're in a temple of madmen! We can't reach Wharton—it's hopeless!"

Jimmy Christopher peered again at the fluttering red drapes. "They are not mad," he answered quietly. "They are united in the hysterical worship of a power they do not understand—of a power that offers them release from the worst fear that the human heart holds. The man who placed that golden crown on his head—that man is holding out to them salvation from—" OPERATOR 5 broke off as the scarlet drapes fluttered anew. They stirred as though the red presence were about to reappear. A hush passed through the temple while every eye watched; but the curtains did not part. Then, again, the powerful voice of the multitude rose, vibrant, compelling, awesome.

Tim Donovan's hand sought Operator 5's. "Jimmy—listen! Do you hear it—back there behind the curtains? That moaning—it's growing louder all the time. First it was only one man—now there're three or four! Jimmy, is it possible—?"

"In this temple tonight, Tim," Jimmy Christopher answered

cryptically, "the impossible is happening. Try not to listen to it, old-timer! Watch Wharton! We've got—"

He broke off again as the crimson curtains once more stirred. This time they parted slowly; this time a red hand reached out into the flickering light of the torches. At its appearance, the voice of the congregation sighed away into silence. As the hush pervaded the temple, a second crimson hand appeared, and the two drew the drapes wide.

The figure robed in the color of blood stepped into the light of the flames. The drapes swung behind him as he paused, peering at the captive chained to the pulpit. Slow steps advanced him. He raised his red hands and his muffled tones carried again through the quiet:

"They await the soul which will raise them from death!"

Utter stillness reigned while the crowned figure reached inside his robe of red. He drew into the wavering light a long-bladed knife. Both his hands gripped its hilt. He raised it slowly while the gleam of the torches played along its sharp edge. He poised it above the body of Hamilton Wharton and his body tensed to drive it down....

"They wait for life! They hunger for this soul! They shall rise from the Darkness when this heart grows still!"

Operator 5 whirled toward the opening in the space behind the organ. He poised, peering across the dais, with Tim Donovan clutching frantically at his arm, with X-11 pressing tensely at his shoulder. His gaze held to the knife raised aloft. He heard a hysterical murmur sweep through the congregation. Out of it rose a shrill cry, swiftly echoed:

"Strike!"

"Give them life—strike!"

"Return them to us, Master! Hail the Master of Death!"

"Strike!"

The blade in the red hands of the crowned figure began to descend....

Jimmy Christopher sprang into the open. Swift steps carried him toward the pulpit where Hamilton Wharton was cringing in terror beneath the lowering blade. His hand shot out to grip the red-sleeved wrist. He pulled the knife aside; he twisted sharply upon the red-gloved fingers and tore the hilt away. He stepped back swiftly, the weapon in his hands.

The crowned figure whirled—and a thunderbolt of wrath shook the walls. From the throats of the hundreds, a savage roar burst. They leaped from their seats in sudden frenzy. The foremost sprang up the steps, crowding upon the dais. Operator 5 whirled to confront grim-faced men who lurched toward him, their eyes glinting with a fanatical anger. On both sides, miners mobbed toward him, enclosing him, trapping him near the pulpit....

A SHARP cry sounded through the uproar: "Jimmy! Jimmy!" from the frantic Tim Donovan. The boy sprang out, driving his fists blindly at the men advancing upon Operator 5. They whipped upon him; they seized his arms in huge, hard hands. Others herded toward the opening of the space behind the organ and sprang upon X-11. They dragged the secret agent out, tearing an automatic from his fingers, thrusting him hard against the wall. Calloused fingers gripped his throat. Hard hands pinioned Tim Donovan. Through the sudden tumult, Jimmy Christopher's voice carried a warning:

"Easy, Tim! Don't resist them! Don't resist!"

He stood poised beside the man chained to the pulpit, facing the figure in crimson. His arms were gripped; he was dragged backward. The man who wore the crown peered at him intently through the eyeholes of the scarlet mask; his muffled voice gave blurted orders. Immediately, the crowd began to leave the platform, except those who held Operator 5 and Tim Donovan and X-11 prisoners.

The Master of Death raised red hands, and the anger of the crowd subsided into silence. In the tense quiet, he turned. His long robe rustled as he glided close to Jimmy Christopher. His red-gloved hands seized the hilt of the knife and he drew it away. His eyes lighted madly, as though a leering smile were hidden by the folds of his crimson mask.

"Perhaps," he said quietly, "you prefer to bequeath your own soul, so that those who died may live again?"

He stepped closer, the glittering knife poised, his blood-red fingers toying with the keen blade.

"We have need for souls—many souls.... We must liberate the souls of disbelievers so that the eternal substance may reenter the bodies of those who have entered the Darkness; so that the faithful may live again and forever! We do not kill those who challenge us. We remove from them all possible promise of resurrection! *We destroy them!*"

The hushed voice dropped to whisper: "Destroy them even as the Master of Death is about to destroy one who dared defy us!"

The man in red turned away sharply. His muffled command moved a man at the rear of the dais. That man stepped forward, lifting a golden bowl from a table, bringing it forward, placing it near the pulpit to which the prisoner was chained. An amber liquid rippled inside it. Into the fluid the Master of Death thrust the blade of the knife. Then again he turned, gripping the hilt in both hands, raising the weapon above the cowering man pinioned to the pulpit.

Again the silence was broken by hysterical cries from the congregation. "Strike!" Again the body of the red-robed man tensed and prepared to drive the blade downward.

"Give his soul to the dead!"

The red figure poised; the knife-blade glinted brightly in the shine of the torches.

"Return them to life! Strike!"

Operator 5 strove to tear from the hands that gripped him—strove against a united strength that held him motionless.

"Strike!"

The blade darted down.

Jimmy Christopher recoiled in horror. He heard a sharp gasp, a lowering moan as the knife drove deep. He closed his eyes instinctively as utter silence returned to the temple. No movement stirred the hush, no breath disturbed the air, for a long moment. Then, at the pulpit, there was a rustle of silk....

Operator 5 peered to see the Master of Death bent above the motionless form. He gazed out upon white faces, into wide eyes, and saw lips parted in awe. In no face was there a suggestion of horror; in every eye there was limitless worship. Each ripple of the silk gown of the Master of Death carried far into the silence. And the silence held until the red-robed figure straightened and whispered:

"They live!"

HE STEPPED back, lifting his hands aloft. He brought them downward swiftly, plunging them into the amber liquid in the golden bowl. He raised them again as a breath passed through the multitude—raised them and held in the light of the flames—a human heart!

High in the air, the Master of Death held the heart of the human sacrifice—*and it beat!*

"They live!"

"They live!"

"THEY LIVE!"

The cry of the Master of Death echoed from the lips of the awe-stricken hundreds. He backed away quickly. He passed through the folds of the crimson curtain. The drapes grew still as the cry was repeated with rising fervor, with hysterical swiftness. Then the curtains began to stir again. The unseen, unfelt wind stirred the folds as the united voice chanted:

"They have come back!"

The curtains began to part. Through them, two grimy hands appeared—hands that began slowly to pull the drapes aside—the calloused hands of a miner….

Operator 5 glanced quickly into the rapt faces of the men who held him prisoner. They were gazing at the curtains with deep fascination. Their eyes saw nothing, their minds were aware of nothing, except those hands appearing from the space beyond.

They were unaware, for the moment, of the man they were holding. Jimmy Christopher seized that opportunity.

He stepped forward swiftly and whirled; he tore his arms free from the loosened fingers. His fists shot out with lightning speed, cracking to the faces of two men who barred his way backward. They spilled aside; others groped confusedly for Operator 5 as he leaped through. He sped across the dais, his hand darting in and out of the loose coveralls. His automatic flashed and two quick shots shook echoes from the musty walls of the desecrated church.

The bullets clicked into the wood beside the heads of the two men gripping Tim Donovan's arms. The boy tore away frantically. He whirled beyond the reach of their groping arms; he sped to Operator 5's side. Again Jimmy Christopher's automatic cracked out bullets that sent two more men leaping aside to safety—the pair who had held X-11 against the paneling. They whirled, backing to the space behind the organ. Operator 5's free hand snatched at the back of a chair and his voice rang sharp:

"Stay there—or be destroyed!"

"Destroyed!"

The word broke in horror from a miner who had lurched after them. He stopped his charge short. Jimmy Christopher sensed Tim Donovan and X-11 crowding into the space behind him. Twice more he fired, sending singing bullets above the heads of the bewildered men on the platform. A quick whirl took him out of sight; a swing of his arm sent the chair twirling powerfully against the red window, with its black-lined crown, behind the organ.

"Out, Tim! Fast!"

Glass shattered outward. Tim Donovan ducked frantically to the jagged sill. X-11's hand jerked unconsciously at his empty armpit holster as he backed to follow. The boy scrambled through, Jimmy Christopher covered the flame-lighted opening with his gun as X-11 poised to follow. He backed as a hoarse cry broke from the platform they had left—a shout in the muffled voice of the Master of Death!

"Destroy them! *Destroy them!*"

IN THE curtained opening, a coveralled man appeared swiftly. In his hand he held an automatic—the weapon he had taken from X-11. He fired swiftly at the window. The bullet whined past Operator 5; a burst of breath sounded behind him, followed at once by the soft thud of a falling body. From the outside, Tim Donovan cried "Jimmy! He's—" and the last word was lost in the explosion of Jimmy Christopher's gun.

The miner with the automatic uttered a sharp shout of pain and whirled away. Operator 5's bullet, tearing into the wrist of the hand that held the gun, drove him backward. Two swift shots from Jimmy Christopher's gun kept the opening clear as he heeled to the sill of the window. He dropped through into the darkness and felt Tim Donovan's small hands grip his arms.

"Jimmy! He's hit!"

"I'll take care of him, Tim! Back along the street! Quick!"

A savage roar burst out inside the red paned windows. A trample of feet sounded as heavy-shoed men crowded toward the doors. Operator 5 thrust the frantic Irish lad away, turned to find X-11 lying motionless beneath the window. The secret agent's face was pasty white, except for a splotch of red in the center of his forehead, a crimson blot surrounding a black hole. The miner's bullet had drilled squarely through X-11's brain.

One instant only Jimmy Christopher hesitated, peering grimly into the face of his dead comrade. Then, as the side door of the church slammed open, he whirled to run through the deep shadows. He leaped across the open space at the rear of the building as men came crowding through. He darted into one doorway and out another; he sprang into a passage that carried him into a cinder yard. He cleared a fence at a running leap, ducked low in darkness at the far corner of the street.

"Tim!"

"Here, Jimmy!"

The tough lad sprang from a doorway nearer the corner. They whirled away together; together they darted into the open space beyond the town. Across the grass slopes above, they heard men running. They saw the moving figures of sentries, scattering at the alarm, and dropped flat. They lay still, scarcely breathing, while the guards rushed down toward the buildings.

"Clear, Tim! Up!"

Jimmy Christopher led the way up the slope, running at a crouch, gun in hand, eyes shifting right and left. They reached a crest of land behind which pooled blackness lay. Just beyond it, they paused, breath beating hotly from their lungs. Through shielding bushes they peered down into the street through which the procession of the dead had recently passed.

Scores of men were running along the sidewalks, carrying cudgels, lighting dark crannies with their torches. Except for the squad undertaking the grim search, the streets were empty. The windows of the desecrated church still radiated light, glowing blood-red, outlining in black the symbol of the crown. From within the walls, the voice of the congregation still rose in its weird, vibrant cry. It seemed to swell to the limits of the night as Operator 5 and Tim Donovan crouched side by side, hidden by the darkness.

The Irish lad exclaimed: "I saw X-11 get hit, Jimmy. Is he—is he—?"

"Killed," Operator 5 answered tersely.

"Killed instantly! There was no time even to—"

Out of the chorus swelling from the Temple of the Crown, words carried—words that held Jimmy Christopher spellbound:

"Gaze upon them! Gaze upon the dead who live again!"

"They have come back!"

"The Darkness has given them up!"

"Raise your voices in joy that the dead have returned!"

Grimly, cautiously, Operator 5 rose. His hand closed upon Tim Donovan's arm: "They'll be coming into the hills after us in a moment, Tim. We've got to leave X-11. We've got to get back—there's no other way. Watch yourself, Tim! Straight back—to the car!"

The boy gazed at Operator 5's dark-lined face shining dimly in the light of the distant torches. "They're saying that those dead men have come back to life! Listen to them, Jimmy! It can't be true! Those men were dead—I saw they were dead!"

"They were dead, Tim. But now—"

His voice trailed off as he started through the darkness. He kept Tim Donovan close at his side as they skirted deep through the wilderness of the night. Behind them, they left the valley where a voice rose in awesome worship of an evil power....

In all that black world of hills, there was no sound save the mighty song that rose from the Temple of the Crown—and, at last, the breathy hum of a powerful motor that faded far into the distance....

CHAPTER 3
WINGS BRING DEATH

P ASSENGERS ALIGHTING from the elevators on the fifty-fourth floor of one of the tallest buildings in New York City entered a quiet, sumptuously furnished reception-room. The directory in the lobby listed these offices as those of the United Eastern Oil Refineries. To the initiated, they were known to be secret Headquarters B-3 of the United States Intelligence Service.

Day and night, men were on duty in inner rooms that were well hidden behind the foyer entrances. No one not in possession of certain passwords, which were changed daily, could penetrate beyond the steel doors. Here, high above the humming streets of Manhattan, corps of secret agents received their orders and gave their reports; here tremendous files, duplicating the master-file at central headquarters WDC-13 in Washington, were kept up to the minute; here the communications-room received and sent dispatches to United States Intelligence men stationed all over the globe. Secretly, twenty-four hours a day, the Intelligence service system functioned smoothly.

A month ago the United Eastern Oil Refiners had not existed; in another month, the name would have vanished off the building directory; but tonight, these offices were the controlling center of scores of undercover men in the metropolis.

In a corner office, far above the peaks of the surrounding buildings, Operator 5 sat at a desk littered with teletyped reports and clipped news dispatches. He had brought many folders from the files lining the walls. For hours, he had sat completely absorbed in the task of correlating the data he had drawn from the metal drawers, while Tim Donovan, sitting silently in a corner, watched him intently. He worked carefully, unconscious of his surroundings.

His fingers strayed to his death's head watch-charm as he read:

… B-3-NY… FOLLOWING INFORMATION NOT GIVEN TO BOSTON PRESS… POLICE HERE MYSTI-FIED BY DISAPPEARANCES OF DEAD BODIES… WITHIN PAST WEEK FOUR HAVE DISAPPEARED… WALTER WHITLEY MERCHANT VANISHED FROM HOME WHERE DEATH OCCURRED… TWO VANISHED FROM UNDERTAKING PARLORS IMME-DIATELY AFTER ARRIVAL… ANOTHER, MILDRED SMYTHE, SUICIDE IN ROOMING HOUSE, DISCOV-ERED BY MAID, DISAPPEARED BEFORE POLICE ARRIVED… NO CLUES… WISHING TO SPARE RELA-

TIVES WORRY POLICE HAVE WITHHELD INFOR-
MATION FROM NEWSPAPERS… BM….

Jimmy Christopher turned to another report, typewritten
and bearing the code-mark indicating that it had originated in
New York City:

… SPECIAL… NO DETAIL… HAVE NOTICED
ON SEVERAL OCCASIONS UNUSUAL VEHICLE
IN STREETS AROUND WATERFRONT DURING
EARLY HOURS OF MORNING… CAR NOT A
PASSENGER BUT PERHAPS A DE LUXE DELIV-
ERY TRUCK COLOR CRIMSON MARKED ONLY
WITH CROWN OUTLINED IN BLACK ON SIDES…
ACTIONS STRANGE… KNOWN TO BE EQUIPPED
WITH RADIO FOR POLICE CALLS… INQUIRIES
RESULTED IN INFORMATION THIS CAR SEEN
HURRIEDLY LEAVING SCENE OF ALARMS AS
PROWL CARS APPEARED… ALARMS OF FIGHTS
PROVE UNFOUNDED AFTER THIS CAR HAS
APPEARED… HAVE ATTEMPTED TO LOCATE
ITS GARAGE WITHOUT SUCCESS… SEAMEN
AT BATTERY SUPERSTITIOUS CONCERNING IT
BELIEVES ITS APPEARANCE MEANS DEATH…
TALES CIRCULATING THAT IT IS MANNED BY
VAMPIRES SEARCHING FOR CORPSES… FURTHER
INVESTIGATION IF REQUESTED… X-11….

The secret agent who had been killed in Carbonville had

filed that report, and across it was stamped the words: *File for Reference.*

Jimmy Christopher lowered the report, his eyes darkened. He lifted a newspaper clipping bearing the date of that day. It had been the first he had read; and now he returned to it with a growing fascination.

CARBONVILLE ISOLATED; WHARTON STILL MISSING; WEIRD RUMORS FROM MINES!

Carbonville, Penn.—Officials of the Wharton Corporation Mines are making every effort to locate Hamilton Wharton, President, but without success. Striking miners are guarding all roads and warning all comers off. Police investigating Wharton's disappearance were outnumbered and turned back. It is understood that the Governor has received appeals for martial law to be established in the coal-mine district.

Rumors circulating from Carbonville state that the six miners entrapped in a vein two days ago have been saved and are alive. This rumor conflicts with a previous report that the victims could not possibly have survived. One reporter was told guardedly that, nevertheless, all six men were well and had returned to their homes today.

THE RASP of a buzzer made Jimmy Christopher raise his darkened eyes. He tipped the cam of the Dictaphone and a voice twanged:

"Operator 5, Z-7 is here!"

Tim Donovan sprang to follow as Operator 5 turned to the

door. Carrying the dispatches, he strode along a corridor to another corner room. He thrust in to find a man clad in gray just removing top-coat and gloves.

"Chief! I've been waiting for you!"

The black eyes of the director of all Intelligence activities of the United States—the man known only as Z-7 even to his most trusted men—searched Operator 5. He seized Jimmy Christopher's hand eagerly.

"I rushed here the moment the plane dropped me at Newark airport. I came as soon as I could possibly leave WDC-13. I've read your report a dozen times. I am frank to say that I am completely bewildered. If anyone but you had submitted it—"

Operator 5 smiled grimly. "You may well believe every word of it, Chief. That report was a statement of bald fact. It means that we're facing the most amazing case we've ever tackled."

Z-7 strode to his desk. He jerked Jimmy Christopher's tele-typed report from his pocket and gazed at it while his fingers drummed. His black eyes gleamed at statements which startled him anew.

"You're positive?" he demanded suddenly. "That man was Hamilton Wharton? You saw him murdered? You actually saw his heart cut from his body—saw it held in the hands of the man who killed him and—*it beat?*"

"I saw exactly that, Chief. It means first of all that the man who is hailed as the Master of Death is a skilled surgeon. He was prepared to make that isolated heart function before the eyes of those in the temple. That in itself is amazing, but medical experiments have accomplished it many times.* This case, Chief, is far more than the murder of one man by another, far more than the spread of a new cult. The Master of Death has discovered a new power—he has taken it into his hands as a

---

* AUTHOR'S NOTE: Lest the reader feel that the following facts, stated baldly, are incredible, I quote from a treatise by G. Anrep, M.A., Lecturer in Physiology at the University of Cambridge:

"The cause of the heart beat has naturally been one of the most continued subjects of inquiry. H. Allen in 1757 was the first to show that the activity of the heart is not dependent on its connections with the nervous system. The heart is controlled and influenced by the nervous system, but this control is not essential for life. The excised heart of a frog continues to beat rhythmically for days, provided that it is supplied with oxygen and prevented from drying. In the case of the warm-blooded animal, the heart is similarly capable of continuing its rhythmic contractions for some time after excision."

The heart, therefore, will continue to beat for a long time, under the proper conditions, after it has been removed from the body!

Again, the same authority, on the subject of the isolated mammalian heart:

"A mammalian heart, which has been removed after the death of an animal, can easily be revived if the coronary arteries are perfused under pressure with blood or a salt solution which resembles the saline medium of the blood in composition. With the use of such a solution, a mammalian heart can be restored to activity as long as seven days after death. The beat of an isolated heart of a child can be restored twenty hours after death from pneumonia. The excised heart of a cat can be kept beating for four days. The heart of a monkey was restored after freezing the dead body of the animal."

These amazing statements are, of course, accepted fact.

weapon. It is a weapon more to be feared than any other which has ever been wielded."

Z-7 studied Jimmy Christopher's face intently. "I know well that your warnings are to be heeded, Operator 5. I realize you never express your conclusions until you are absolutely sure of them. But exactly what do you mean?"

"I mean, Chief," Jimmy Christopher answered, "that this man, whom I saw hailed last night as the Master of Death, has conceived a plan of gigantic proportions. He has already taken the first steps to put it into operation. He has begun slowly, carefully, on a small scale. Already he completely dominates and rules that mining town. The people there are his worshipful slaves. I am positive, Chief, that it is his intention to spread his uncanny power until—"

"His power—his weapon?" Z-7 questioned grimly. "I am still mystified. What are these things?"

"The power of fear, Chief—a fear that is rooted deep in the heart of every human being, the strongest fear that rules the mind: The fear of death! The Master of Death is using that fear as his weapon by eliminating it from the minds of those who pledge themselves to him—by strengthening it in the minds of those who challenge him. He is making slaves of his followers with a force greater than gold, greater than any other in the world. His is a promise of everlasting life!"

Z-7 GESTURED impatiently. "Yes—but he cannot fulfill that promise. He cannot wholly wipe that fear out of the human mind. Death is a force he cannot actually conquer. As soon as his followers learn this, his plan will collapse of its own falseness."

Operator 5 smiled tightly. "You underestimate the talent of the Master of Death, Chief. I can understand why you are skeptical of his power. You cannot realize the full danger of this situation until you do understand it. You've got to try to grasp it, Chief. You've got to realize that this man is one who has actually conquered death!"

Z-7 stared; he smiled wryly. "I deal in facts. I'm a hard-headed realist. This Intelligence service would accomplish nothing if it were not able to differentiate fact from rumor, truth from fancy. I am trying to follow your reasoning, but so far there is no evidence to prove—"

"Chief," Operator 5 leaned tensely over the desk, "I also am dealing in facts. For a long time, I have been gathering information on this very subject. I have been forced to these conclusions, Chief—*forced* to them!

"I believe implicitly that the robed man I saw last night has conquered death at least temporarily. I believe that unless we destroy him, he will destroy us!"

Z-7 came to his feet. "You feel sure," he demanded, "that the

JIMMY CHRISTOPHER.

so-called Master of Death possesses the power to make the dead live again?"

"Yes, Chief—to a dangerous extent. He is able to restore life to a body if its mechanism has not been destroyed. He can cause a dead heart to beat again, dead lungs to breathe again, dead eyes to see and dead lips to speak."

A shrill ring of a telephone bell interrupted Jimmy Christopher. Z-7 stood gazing at him in fascination, unaware of the summons until it was repeated. He lifted the telephone slowly; he listened to a voice that came rasping over the wire.

Suddenly he blurted: "Men wearing—what? You're sure of that? Yes! Watch yourself, R-4! Stay there in the loft! Wait for us!"

The Washington chief lowered the instrument to peer at Operator 5.

"The symbol of the crown!" he exclaimed. "Your report speaks of it—on the shrouds, on the windows of that defiled church— the mark of the Master of Death! R-4 is on duty at Loft C and he declares he has seen men watching the place; men wearing a golden ornament in their lapels—a crown!"

Operator 5's eyes narrowed. "My roadster's outside, Chief. I suggest that we get the full details from R-4 immediately." His voice fell to a whisper: "Men wearing the—symbol of the crown!"

He turned to the door quickly. Tim Donovan strode at his side; with Z-7 they entered the quiet foyer. They did not speak while the elevator dropped them to the lobby of the building. They strode together to the sleek roadster parked in the side-street.

With Operator 5 at the wheel, with Tim Donovan wedged between him and Z-7, they turned north. The Washington chief frowned gravely. As they hurried past intersections, he quietly said:

"You saw those six men carried into the church, my boy, but you did not see them reappear?"

"I heard the congregation chanting that the dead men *had* reappeared, Chief."

"They were deluded, then," Z-7 declared vehemently. "The Master of Death must wield some hypnotic power which makes his followers see things which do not exist. Or, if those men did actually reappear alive, they were not dead in the first place. The gas they breathed while trapped in the mine shaft must have brought about a condition of catalepsy, so that they seemed dead but were actually alive."

"Those men, Chief," Operator 5 declared firmly, "were not in a condition of suspended animation. I'm positive of that. They were dead—actually dead!"

"Great Scott!" Z-7 exclaimed. "If what you say happened actually took place, nothing is impossible."

Jimmy Christopher swung the roadster to the curb. They approached a small apartment-house on the West side, not far from the Hudson. An ancient elevator lifted them to the top floor. At a fastened door, Z-7, still absorbed in thought, knocked. They waited a silent moment.

"Strange," the Washington chief mused. "R-4 must be here. I asked him to wait."

Quietly Operator 5 suggested: "Your keys, Chief?"

Z-7 drew a pack of keys from his pocket and inserted one in the lock. He opened the way upon a narrow flight of stairs which ascended through the roof to another door. He knocked again, and when no answer came he used his keys again. Oper-  ator 5 stepped with him, and Tim Donovan followed, into a narrow hallway.

The superstructure consisted of two rooms, both of which were now closed. It housed Loft C of the Intelligence Service—a station devoted to the training of carrier pigeons. The loft, as well as several others in New York, was maintained so that the birds might be used in emergencies; an undercover agent was in continual attendance. Yet, when Z-7 tried one of the doors and found it locked, when he knocked loudly and called for R-4, there was no answer.

HIS BLACK eyes smoldering with uncertainty, he opened the way into the front room. Operator 5 entered a small office in which were a desk, a chair, and files containing the flight reports on the pigeons kept here. He paused, gazing at the telephone on the desk. It was overturned; the receiver was off the hook. He strode to the connecting door, thrust it open wide—and stopped short.

The room was walled with cages—scores of them, provided for keeping the pigeons. Ordinarily, each mesh-enclosed space was aflutter with wings; ordinarily the room was busy with the excited chirping of the birds. Now there was no sound. Now there was no bird visible. Every door of every cage was open—and the cages were empty.

In the center of the floor lay a body—a body without a head!

Z-7 blurted: "Great God!" and strode in. His face paled as he peered down at the decapitated cadaver—at the ugly red blot on the floor. Beside the raw stump of the neck, the floor was gashed deep, as if from the blow of a heavy, sharp-bladed weapon. In ghastly silence, Z-7 and Operator 5 peered at the body; wide-eyed Tim Donovan recoiled from it.

Operator 5 stooped to search the floor. He scanned every inch of it, and straightened grimly. His lips tightened as he said in a whisper: "R-4—but the head is missing!" Operator 5 glanced at the rear of the room, where two broad casement windows stood open and unscreened; they looked across the black rectangle of the roof, upon the lights of the city twinkling beyond. In front of them a table stood; and Jimmy Christopher moved toward it. His eyes narrowed at an object which stood in the shine of light.

It was a crude earthen image, six inches high. The gray clay gave the face a sinister cast. Its arms were extended as if for an embrace. And on its base a numeral was freshly inscribed—the figure 2.

"In God's name!" Z-7 blurted. "What is that thing?"

Operator 5 quickly drew a pair of black gloves from his pocket. He lifted the graven image and signaled Z-7 to follow him. They reentered the office; Jimmy Christopher closed the door. With his gloved hand, he returned the telephone instrument to its standard.

"R-4 must have been attempting to call headquarters again, Chief, when he was attacked."

"By the wearers of the golden crown!"

"Without doubt! They overpowered R-4; they carried every pigeon away. They are planning to use those birds for some devilish purpose—depend on that, Chief! We've got to do everything possible to trace them. Call B-3! We can't waste time!"

Z-7 quickly drew on gloves and raised the telephone as Operator 5 circled the room.

"Get half a dozen men here as soon as possible," Operator 5 directed. "The elevator operator must be questioned. Every square inch of these two rooms must be gone over for fingerprints. This image, if possible, must be traced."

Z-7 spoke rapidly into the instrument. Tim Donovan stared side-eyed at the little clay statue in the hands of Operator 5. He blurted breathlessly: "What is it, Jimmy? It looks horrible!"

"It is horrible, Tim," Jimmy Christopher agreed. "It is the image of a deity in Vedic Hindu mythology. It is an image of Yama—the King of the Dead! Yama! Remember, Tim, the first word we heard the Master of Death utter last night—the very first. *Yajna!* That, too"

Z-7 stopped speaking abruptly as he completed issuing orders to headquarters B-3. Operator 5 broke off. Tim Donovan's eyes widened as he listened. A single sound came into the silence of the superstructure. It penetrated the closed door of the loft, faint, uncanny.

It was a scratching, a chirping, a fluttering of wings.

OPERATOR 5'S hand shot to the knob. He stepped through

alertly and again stopped short. The rustle, the squeaking became louder with the opening of the door. Z-7 and Tim Donovan paused behind him as he peered across the room—at a lone pigeon.

It was clinging to the mesh of one of the cages; its claws were scratching the wires and its feathers glistened with a bright sheen. Operator 5 gently closed his hand around it. He brought it close and saw that a tiny aluminum cylinder was tied with thread to each of its legs; that it carried an identification band.

"USI-98!" Jimmy Christopher read. "It's one of our birds, chief! It must have been released only a short time ago by the men who stole all the pigeons and murdered R-4!"

"It's carrying a message!" Z-7 explained.

"A message—yes! Perhaps more than a message," Jimmy Christopher said quietly.

He held the bird as Tim Donovan deftly removed one of the tiny cylinders from the bird's legs. The boy drew its halves apart, while Operator 5 watched alertly; a tightly rolled paper came into view. The boy unrolled it quickly. His eyes widened as he held it so that Jimmy Christopher could read the terse message:

FOLLOW ME TO ETERNAL LIFE—ELSE PLUNGE INTO THE EVERLASTING DARKNESS.

And beneath, delicately outlined, a symbolic signature was affixed—a golden crown!

Operator 5 raised darkening eyes. "His weapon is reaching out. Chief—a weapon of horrible fear and devilish promise! His plan is working—now, tonight! He will use that weapon to drive us all into slavery unless—"

Jimmy Christopher broke off as Tim Donovan detached the second of the aluminum cylinders. Attempting to draw the halves apart, the boy exerted more strength than before. Quietly Operator 5 tossed the bird into one of the cages. His dark gaze held to the tiny case in Tim Donovan's fingers. The boy pulled harder and suddenly the halves parted with a resonant report.

"Back!" Operator 5 shouted the warning as he struck out. He swept the tube from Tim Donovan's fingers. He thrust the boy backward and whirled, jerking at Z-7's arm. A pungency came into the air—so slight that only Operator 5 sensed it—as he frantically thrust the Irish lad and the Washington chief to the door. He shouldered them through, warning: "Don't breathe!" He slapped the door shut and stood tense, his face pale, his eyes burning grimly.

"Stay out of that room," he commanded sharply, "if you want to live!"

Startled, Z-7 stared and listened. There was silence beyond the panels again. The fluttering of wings was not audible; the high-pitched voice of the pigeon had ceased. Jimmy Christopher quickly drew a carpet to cover the lower crack of the door.

"Warn your men to stay out of there for at least three hours, chief! If any of them goes in before that gas has had a chance to dissipate, he'll die on the spot!"

"In God's name—what was in that tube?" Z-7 demanded breathlessly.

"Lewisite!* Whoever liberated that bird intended that poison gas to kill us. That pigeon was liberated close to this building by someone who saw us enter. The Master of Death is behind it; he intended that our deaths should strengthen his weapon of fear!" **TIM DONOVAN** stared wide-eyed as Operator 5 picked up the telephone. Quickly Jimmy Christopher called a number, that of his father's home. As he waited, Z-7 exclaimed: "The pigeon was killed almost instantly!"

"That gas, chief," Operator 5 answered tightly, "destroys lung tissue. One killed by it could never live again! Hello! Diane!"

Over the wire, a girl's voice answered: "Jimmy, hello! I've been waiting to hear from you! You've kept so busy that I scarcely see you any more and—"

"Busy, Di," Operator 5 answered, "on the most important case I've ever tackled. I want your help on an important job."

Diane Elliot, a special reporter for the far-flung Amalgamated Press, had assisted Operator 5 in several important cases in the past. Though she was in her early twenties, she had won an enviable position through sheer ability. Jimmy said quietly, while Tim Donovan and Z-7 listened anxiously:

---

* AUTHOR'S NOTE: Lewisite, sometimes called "Death Dew," or in chemical terminology dichlorasine vinylchloride, is one of the deadliest poison gases ever created. It was perfected by Professor Lewis of Northwestern University, Chicago, and large quantities were manufactured in preparation for an air offensive by the Entente planned for 1919, which never occurred. Three drops of Lewisite coming in contact with the skin of a man are sufficient to cause his speedy death.

"I want you to make an appointment for an interview—as a reporter, Di. Please telephone Dr. Anton Kalmar at once—his home is on Long Island. We must see him tonight if possible. Arrange it as soon as you can. I'm coming home at once."

"Certainly, Jimmy! I've already met Dr. Kalmar and interviewed him. I'm sure I can do it. I'll wait for you here."

Operator 5 turned briskly from the telephone. "That's an important lead, chief. Dr. Kalmar is one of only three scientists in the United States who can give me the information I need. Another is Dr. Robert E. Cornish, at the University of California. The other is Dr. Ernest Martin Chesterly. Dr. Chesterly, I learned this afternoon, is at this moment returning from Europe. If Dr. Kalmar is able—"

"Information," Z-7 questioned, "on the resurrection of the dead?"

"Exactly! Chief, our pigeons were stolen from this loft because they are a means of carrying messages to us—a means extremely difficult to trace. "We've got to tackle the job of finding those pigeons. More of them are sure to be liberated from time to time. Possibly they'll carry their messages at night, in order to make tracing them even more difficult, but we've got to make the attempt.

"The service is to charter two autogyros at once—autogyros because they are able to remain stationary in the air and to fly far more slowly than airplanes. Put one of our best agents in each of them as an observer. He is to fly directly above this building and to remain on watch with binoculars. He is to watch for another bird to appear. If he spots it, he's to note the direction of its flight and take a new position farther out along that line. The autogyros will spell each other, and by that means, we may he able to reach out to the spot where those birds have been taken."

Operator 5 stood silent in thought as Z-7 again put through a telephone call. He moved to the outer door, eyes darkened, lips pressed hard, peering toward the room in which deadly gas lurked, where the headless cadaver of a murdered comrade lay. He said nothing until Z-7 came to his side:

"We have made one important discovery, Chief. The Master of Death does not kill his enemies. He destroys them—destroys them so that they may never live again!"

CHAPTER 4
MANSION OF MANIACS

IN FRONT of a modest brownstone house in the East Forties of Manhattan—designated Address Y in the lexicon of the United States Intelligence service—Operator 5 brought his roadster to the curb. He entered with Tim Donovan; he climbed the steps into a quiet living room. As he entered, a mild-mannered man strode to meet him.

"Happy to see you, son!" John Christopher exclaimed. He had once been designated Operator Q-6 in the Intelligence service; a vital wound had forced him to abandon his strenuous duties. Two bullets were embedded so close to his heart that no surgeon had ever dared operate to remove them; they threatened him continually with sudden death. His pride was unbounded in the fact that his son was carrying on his work so admirably.

His hand-clasp was warm, lingering. "Tim has told me of this new case. It fascinates me, Jimmy; it haunts me."

"It has already fascinated hundreds to the point of making them vassals of the Master of Death, Dad." He glanced around quickly. "Where's Di?"

"She rushed off to the office to arrange the interview; she'll be right back," John Christopher answered.

Jimmy Christopher studied his father's face intently—and a darkness grew in his eyes. His fingers strayed to the death symbol on his watch-chain as he strode to the telephone. He saw John Christopher sink into a chair and become lost in thought; and he called the number of secret Intelligence headquarters B-3. An exchange of signals took place: "United Eastern?"

"You have the wrong number."

"Mr. Weston, please."

"We have no Mr. Southern." Operator 5's voice dropped to a whisper: "Z-7, please."

The voice of the Washington chief responded after a moment. "Operator 5, our men are at Loft C, waiting for the gas to dissipate in the rear room and going over the front one now for fingerprints. The one autogyro is already taking its position. The hunt will be continued without a break, according to your orders."

"Good, Chief! In the meantime, our files must be searched. Every report of a vanished dead body must be investigated. We must look for signs of an elaborate espionage system in Operation—an organization of spies whose business it is to locate those who have just died. Every death means a possible candidate for the ranks of the Master of Death—a new slave to do his bidding. Search thoroughly, Chief, and—"

"THERE IS a report on my desk at the moment which is exactly the information you are seeking!" Z-7 exclaimed. "It came over the wires only a few moments ago from the customs office. A box supposedly containing a statue attracted the suspicions of the officials when it was unloaded from the S.S. *Ultima* this evening. Gas was seen to be issuing from it—supposedly carbon dioxide. The box itself is very cold. It was partly opened. It contains—not a statue—but a dead body!"

"A body sent from Europe, chief?" Operator 5 demanded. "Then learn everything possible about it! Check the shipment address. Try to learn the identity of the corpse. But hold it there—hold it until I have had a chance to look at it. It may be a lead, chief—a direct lead to the Master of Death!

"Further, chief, communicate with all police headquarters in the country and try to learn if any others of the little images of Yama have been discovered. Send me to Carbonville in an attempt to find new leads."

As Operator 5 replaced the receiver, and gazed again anxiously at John Christopher, quick footfalls sounded on the stairs. Diane Elliot's voice called "Jimmy!" and she ran eagerly into the room. She flung her arms around Jimmy Christopher's neck; she pressed her warm lips to his. He backed away with his face suffused with mounting color.

"Lord, Di—you overwhelm me!" He smiled into her alert, sparkling eyes. "How about the interview?"

Diane answered, "It's all fixed, Jimmy. In fact, we've got to hurry if we're to get there in time. Dr. Kalmar said he's leaving the city tonight and he can give us only a few minutes. He was reluctant—but I insisted."

"Good girl! We're leaving right now." He strode toward the door, pulling on his hat, and paused to smile at the anxious Tim Donovan. "As for you, Tim—"

"You're not going to leave me behind!" the boy pleaded.

"No, you're coming with us, Tim—I may need you," Jimmy Christopher smiled. He chuckled as the boy grabbed for his cap; but he grew serious again as he turned to John Christopher.

DR. ANTON KALMAR

Ex-Operator Q-6 was gazing into space, scarcely conscious of anything around him. "Dad."

John Christopher jerked back. "Yes, Jimmy?"

"Take it easy, Dad. In case Z-7 'phones any reports, take them, will you?"

John Christopher smiled wanly. "Of course, Jimmy," he said quietly. "Of course…."

Dark lines shone on Operator 5's forehead as he went down the stairs with Diane and Tim. They entered the roadster, and Jimmy Christopher hesitated, gazing at the shining windows of his father's home. His lips tightened as he started the motor and meshed the gears.

THE ROADSTER sped with the wind along a dark, outlying road on upper Long Island. Its headlamps played through blackness that blanketed an unsettled section. Houses were few. The bustle of the metropolis was left far behind. And since Operator 5 had skirted over the Queensboro Bridge, spanning the East River, he had not spoken.

Diane Elliot asked quietly as the roadster rushed on: "You haven't said a word, you've been so preoccupied. You're more worried than I've ever seen you before."

"I'm up against intangible forces—yet they are forces of terrific power," Operator 5 explained. "No one is safe from them—no one. And they are wielded by a man who is completely merciless. He will stop at absolutely nothing to achieve his purpose—I'm sure of that. He has launched a plan so gigantic—If he succeeds in putting his plan into operation, the democracy of the United States will cease to exist!"

Diane Elliot's arm curled through Operator 5's. "You can stop him, Jimmy Christopher!"

Operator 5's head wagged. "I'll try my best, but this is the toughest case I've ever tackled. I'm facing the job alone. Not even Z-7 is convinced of the facts I've told him. I'm on a strange lead tonight. Dr. Kalmar can confirm my contentions. He knows, as few men in the advanced fields of science know, that 'natural' death is an unnatural thing."

"Since Tim told me about what happened last night, Jimmy," the girl said eagerly, "I've dug into the files at the office. There

54

are certain dispatches I scarcely noticed at the time—but now they mean much. Each shows that science has begun to control the forces of death. The use of artificial blood in blood transfusions, for instance—"

"Exactly, Di! And that is far less startling than other facts I expect to learn. I'm positive that the Master of Death has discovered and is withholding a secret which is far in advance of any yet announced in scientific circles—a secret so amazing that it promises its holder greater power than any other man ever held in the history of the world!"

Operator 5's lips pressed hard; he touched the brakes as lights appeared around a bend. Rolling the car toward a stone-posted gate, he observed a name-plate in the shine of the headlamps: *Dr. Anton Kalmar.* Pausing, he spoke quickly to Tim Donovan.

"Slip out, old-timer. Duck out of sight across the road. I want you to watch this place while we're inside. Find out if possible whether or not it's guarded. Don't let yourself be seen."

The Irish lad left the car hurriedly. Operator 5 saw Tim slip out of sight behind a stone fence across the road. He swung into the driveway, turning toward the house which sat screened from the road by heavy trees. With Diane, he approached the entrance and knocked. They waited in a brooding silence, sensing a strange tension in the air, until the entrance clicked open.

A BROAD-SHOULDERED man appeared silhouetted against the light; it emphasized the hollows of his cheeks, the protruding ridge above his eyes. His basilisk stare turned from the girl to Operator 5, and he did not speak.

"We have an appointment to interview Dr. Kalmar."

The answer was in a peculiarly hollow, breathy voice. "Dr. Kalmar will see you in the library."

Jimmy Christopher and the girl followed the thick-shouldered man along a corridor. Diane's lips pursed in puzzlement; she peered intently into the gaunt face as the library door opened. As though struggling for an elusive memory, she absently took a chair beside a broad desk. The square-shouldered man bowed and said throatily:

"I am Karant, Dr. Kalmar's secretary. The Doctor will be here presently. Please wait."

The man who called himself Karant withdrew with a slow, gliding step. Before he closed the door, a murmur reached Operator 5's ears—a sound as of muttering voices, mingling in a closed space somewhere beyond. The door shut to silence the library; Diane Elliot leaned close.

"I've seen that man somewhere before, Jimmy. I'm trying to remember where. He—something about him makes my flesh crawl. His face is like a mummy's. I know I've seen—"

A rattle of the knob broke into the girl's words. A lean man strode into the room hurriedly. His face was narrow and pointed; his eyes were a brilliant gray beneath a bulging forehead. His hair was bushy and unkempt; the hand he extended toward Diane and Operator 5 was cold, bony. He searched their faces as he took the chair on the opposite side of the desk; and immediately he was immobile.

"I am Dr. Kalmar. You wish an interview. On what subject, may I ask?"

"On a subject which only a few men in the world understand," Operator 5 answered. "The resurrection of the dead."

Dr. Kalmar's expression did not change. "Well?"

"It is true, is it not," Operator 5 went on briskly, "that the problem of reviving the dead has occupied scientists for many years. I refer to Crile and Hyman.* New experiments are being

---

* AUTHOR'S NOTE: Thirty years ago, Dr. George Washington Crile, the famous physician of Cleveland, Ohio, undertook experiments to resurrect dead dogs, using saline solutions, chest massages and adrenalin. He succeeded in restoring the beating of the heart, which ceased after a few moments due to clotting of the blood.

Similar experiments were conducted in 1929 at the Mayo Clinic. The experimenters found it was possible to induce hearts to beat which had been motionless for long periods by forcing fluid through them.

Dr. Albert Solomon Hyman, of the Witkin Foundation for the Study and Prevention of Heart Disease, in Manhattan, developed another means of resurrection intended primarily for victims of shock. This method prods the dead heart to act by means of an electrical current. The apparatus used, called a Hymanotor, makes use of a hollow, gold plated needle which is thrust into the right auricle of the dead heart. Into this hollow needle an insulated wire is inserted, completing the circuit to the heart. A generator supplies the current. It was found in the earliest experiments with the Hymanotor that in six cases out of ten the heart could be induced to resume beating if it had not been dead for more than twelve minutes. The practicality of this device is testified by the fact that Dr. Walter Vaughan Hagen took two Hymanotors on his Darwinian Centennial Expedition to the Galapagos Islands, chiefly for the purpose of reviving any members of the expedition

carried on in the field constantly. You are one of the three men in the United States who have carried them farther than any other scientists. Drs. Chesterly and Cornish are the others."

"The resurrection of the dead," Dr. Kalmar said in clipped syllables, "is an accomplished fact. I am referring, of course, to the resuscitation of lower animals. All medical men and many laymen know of the experiments of Dr. Cornish. The first dog which he successfully revived—he named the animal Lazarus* has become famous."

who might be stung by the deadly scorpions infesting the islands, which cause paralysis of the heart.

The most famous and most recent experiments in resurrection, made by Dr. Robert E. Cornish of the University of California, who first attacked the problem of reviving the dead in 1932, have been carried on with the aid of CWA funds.

* AUTHOR'S NOTE: The following is the medical log of "Lazarus," the dog which became famous by living again after having been put to death by Dr. Robert E. Cornish. On Friday, April 13, 1934, Dr. Cornish began giving ether to the dog—the time, 3:58 p.m.—which resulted in his death. The events preceding and following the death of Lazarus:

Heart-beat, 130 per minute, normal. (The smaller the animal the faster the heart-beat. A rat has a normal heart-beat of 400 per minute, while that of a healthy man is about 76.) 3:58 P.M., administration of ether began. 4:01, the dog was unconscious. 4:06, the dog's breathing ceased. 4:08, there was no heart-beat, no pulse, the blood pressure was zero—the dog was dead. 4:11, artificial respiration was begun. 4:12, solution began, 4:12½, the heart began beating. 4:16, heart-beat 220 per mimite as a result of severe shock.

"There is no doubt," Operator 5 inquired, "that in the case of Lazarus, the dog was actually dead, and actually brought back to life?"

"No doubt whatever." Dr. Kalmar answered with clipped accents.

"And these experiments have developed to a point at which it has become possible to resurrect human beings?"

DR. KALMAR'S thin lips curved quickly into a mirthless smile; as suddenly the smile vanished again. "The resurrection of humans is a goal yet to be attained. Such experiments go forward under extremely heavy handicaps, not the least of which is the supply of corpses. So far, every attempt to resurrect a human being has failed."

Operator 5's eyes narrowed. "But it is true that Dr. Cornish,

---

4:38, heart-beat normal, 130 per minute. 10:30 P.M., gum arabic solution, 50 C.C., injected. 10:38, heart-beat 156.

Saturday, April 14. 12:40 A.M., heart-beat 128. 5:50 A.M., heart-beat, 128. 9:00, heart beat 132. 10:15, heart-beat 156. 11:00, heart-beat 168. This constituted a major crisis and Dr. Cornish believed that his subject would die a second time. Saline solution, 300 C.C., was given in a subcutaneous injection. 10:05 P.M., heart-beat 220. 1:08, heart-beat 176. 1:40, heart-beat 164. 6:08, heart-beat 140. 8:20, heart-beat 120.

Sunday, April 15. 7:00 A.M., heart-beat 160; gum arabic solution again injected. 8:30 A.M., heart-beat normal, 130. Since that date the normal heart-beat has been maintained in Lazarus, and the dog increased daily in strength and intelligence. At the present writing he is still living and seems little the worse for his experience.

for instance, now has sufficient confidence in his technique to attempt the resurrection of a human being if the opportunity is given him?"

"He has made some move in that direction, I believe, but nothing has come of it—up until the present time, at least."*

"You have not yourself made such experiments on human beings, Dr. Kalmar?"

"No." The word was flat, final.

"Do you know of any scientist, aside from Drs. Cornish and Chesterly, who is experimenting along these lines—who may have developed his technique to an unparalleled point, who is capable now of resurrecting human beings?"

"I know of no such man."

Jimmy Christopher straightened and studied Dr. Kalmar's implacable face. On sudden decision he removed a silver case from his pocket. He held it before the doctor, his thumbnail touching one corner. Quietly he said:

"I am going to lay my cards on the table, Dr. Kalmar. I am

---

* AUTHOR'S NOTE: Under this headline:

REFUSE PERMISSION TO REVIVE DEAD MEN, the following dispatch appeared recently in newspapers:

"San Francisco, Oct. 15—Dr. Robert E. Cornish of the University of California, who recently revived a dog which had been put to death clinically, proposed today that he continue his experiments on the bodies of executed criminals. Dr. Cornish wrote to the Governors of three states asking if they would permit him to attempt to resuscitate convicts put to death by gas. The officials of the three states, however, frowned on the idea."

not after a newspaper story. I want information for another purpose, a thousand times more important. It involves many serious crimes but, most important of all, I fear it threatens the welfare of the United States. My credentials, sir."

A pressure of Operator 5's thumbnail, and a leaf sprang open in the silver case. The doctor's eyes flickered with surprise and he leaned forward to read the document framed inside it. His eyes brightened to amazing intensity as they followed the few terse lines,

THE WHITE HOUSE
Washington

To Whom It May Concern:
The identity of the bearer of this letter must be kept strictly confidential.
He is Operator 5 of the United States Intelligence Service.

The signature was that of the President of the United States.

Quietly, firmly, Operator 5 said: "I ask you again, Dr. Kalmar, if you know of any scientist who has brought the technique of resurrecting human beings to the point of absolute perfection?"

"I do not!"

Slowly Jimmy Christopher returned the silver case to his pocket. His darkening eyes did not leave the inscrutable face of Dr. Kalmar. Quietly he persisted:

"Is it not true that Dr. Cornish, years ago, attempted the resurrection of a dead man—that this attempt might have succeeded if he had then been in possession of data which he has since obtained through experiments on lower animals?" *

* AUTHOR'S NOTE: From medical records in San Francisco, the following data on an early attempt to resurrect a human being has been obtained. Note that tire failure is obviously due to faulty technique. Even at that date, February 4, 1933, improvements in technique promised successful results. From the record:

"W.G., age 62, a printer, applied for treatment at Center Emergency Hospital, San Francisco. He was given a room and found dead in same about thirty minutes later: death listed as 'cardiac failure.' Body put in ice box for some time; teeter-board test started about 4½ hours after finding body. Test continued 1½ hours. The arms and legs were very cold; application of electric heating pads did not adequately reheat these parts. No evidence in circulation of limbs (by distension of surface veins). Head veins showed distension when head was lowered. About the middle of the test, face seemed to warm up suddenly; sparkle returned to eyes and pulsations were observed in soft tissue between windpipe and sternum—*i.e.*, in the hollow formed by the two front collar-bones. Frequency of pulsations about 70 per minute; these pulsations tended to die away but were revived again by each tipping of the teeter-board. This was probably due to heart beats. Desperate attempts were made then to produce artificial respiration but stiffness of ribs (due to cold) and blocking of windpipe could not be combated with available equipment. After about ten minutes, no more pulsations could be produced, face rapidly cooled, sparkle disappeared from eyes and distension of head veins when lowered became much less. Lips also changed expression at this moment, and a rotation of the eyeballs was noted."

"That experiment, as you must know," Dr. Kalmar answered with a snap, "failed! That is the scientific fact."

OPERATOR 5'S fingers strayed slowly to the death-charm on his watch-chain. His voice took on an edge as he pressed his line of thought:

"Is it not true that Dr. Brjuchenenko, of the Central Institute of Blood Transfusion in Moscow, almost succeeded, only recently, in the resurrection of a human being who had been dead three hours?"*

Dr. Kalmar's eyes blazed. "That experiment also failed. I repeat: there have been no successful resurrections of dead human beings."

* AUTHOR'S NOTE: Under the headline LIFE RESTORED TO DEAD MAN, the following news dispatch was cabled to the United States by the United Press from Moscow under date of October 30 last:

"The first known instance of a revival of a human being actually dead was reported today by a high Soviet authority.

"The Central Institute of Blood Transfusion, which has conducted numerous experiments in reviving animals, claimed it had recently restored life for two minutes in a man who had been dead for three hours after committing suicide by hanging.

"Animation was said to have been restored by means of the 'artificial heart' invented by Professor Sergei Brjuchenenko of the Institute.

"After the artificial heart had been pumping blood for some minutes, the man purportedly began breathing and showed other signs of life for about two minutes and then died again."

"On the contrary, Dr. Kalmar," Jimmy Christopher asserted quietly, "there have been!"

Dr. Kalmar jerked to his feet. The pastiness of his face became more pronounced. The brilliance of his eyes was a gleam of ferocity. "Do you, a layman, presume to contradict a man who has devoted years—?"

"Last night," Jimmy Christopher interrupted sharply, "six dead men were restored to life. Six men who had died of suffocation were made to breathe again—and there were hundreds of witnesses! Do you know of that, Dr. Kalmar?"

From the dry, thin lips came an explosive: "No!" And as the word burst out, a quick knocking sounded—a frantic sound on the panels of the library door.

At Dr. Kalmar's sharp call the man who called himself Karant entered. The secretary hesitated, glancing fearfully at Operator 5; he strode forward in extreme agitation, his hands fluttering, his eyes widened. He stepped to the desk and blurted:

"Beg pardon, sir! An emergency, sir!"

Into the shine of the desk-lamp, he thrust a message which he had written on a slip of paper. During the moment of tense quiet there stole into the room the same sounds Jimmy Christopher had heard before—a labial mumbling, as from a closed space, though now it was louder, rising to a hysterical pitch. Listening to it, Jimmy Christopher gazed at the slip of paper in the light—and his eyes sharpened.

THE GLEAM of the lamp shone through the slip, and the message, in reverse, was visible to Operator 5. It read cryptically:

No. 3 has escaped!

Dr. Kalmar whirled from the desk. The smock he was wearing flicked away from his long legs as he strode rapidly to the door. Karant followed him out; the secretary gave an appalled backward glance as he closed the door. Into the room, silence came again.

Diane Elliot turned anxiously to Jimmy Christopher. Her face was lighted; words were trembling on her lips, as though she feared to utter them. Suddenly she leaned forward. Her whisper was breathless:

"Jimmy! It seems impossible—but I'm sure! I remember that secretary now. His name is Walter Jens. A year ago, he was a teller in the Engineers' National Bank. He disappeared for a few days, then Jimmy, I remember it perfectly! I saw the story go out over the wires, and I saw his photograph. There's no possible mistake, but—"

"Go on, Di," Operator 5 asked grimly. "And after he disappeared—?"

"His body was found in the East River! He'd committed suicide over family troubles. Months ago! Months ago, Jimmy, that man died! He died, but he's here now—alive!"

Jimmy Christopher's eyes were blazing. "Karant," he mused slowly. "Karant.... Phonetically, that name is the same as the French word meaning 'forty.' Forty! Number Forty! And Number Three has just—"

Quick footfalls sounded in the hallway; the door snapped open. Dr. Anton Kalmar strode into the library. Beneath his heavy brows, his eyes were fiery. He stopped short just inside the door, breathing quickly, his hand twined hard on the knob.

"My pardon," he said rapidly. "I regret that the interview is finished. A highly important matter.... You will leave at once. Karant—show them—"

He broke off, gesturing frantically. He hurried out of sight down the corridor. In the doorway the secretary remained, his face shadowed gauntly, his eyes wide and peering. Diane Elliot stared at him in cold fascination. Operator 5 strode to the door and paused there a moment.

"We know the way to the door," he said quietly, "Mr. Jens."

The haggard face did not change expression. The wide eyes betrayed no astonishment. The box-shouldered man merely stood, staring, breathless, as he had a moment before.

"Jens is not my name. I am Karant I am sorry—you must leave immediately. It is most important! A crisis in the laboratory—"

"I quite understand." Jimmy Christopher's eyes narrowed thoughtfully as he strode past. He escorted Diane Elliot to the door. They crossed the porch and entered the car. When the motor was humming, Operator 5 glanced back at the entrance, sensing a frantic activity beyond, an electrical tightness in the air. "We have talked," he said with quiet conviction, "with a man who once was dead!"

CHAPTER 5
WHILE DEAD EYES WATCHED

OPERATOR 5 sent the roadster rolling to the stone gate. Slowing, he glanced back. Far beyond the trees shading the house he saw moving shapes. Out of the gloom flickered the gleam of flashlights. From the bushes of the gardens came rustling sounds, as of men brushing them aside in frantic search. A calling voice reached through the humming of the Diesel motor—the high-pitched tones of Dr. Kalmar.

"Quick! Shut the gate! Watch all the fence!"

Diane Elliot's hand tightened on Jimmy Christopher's arm as he turned into the road. He glanced at the spot where Tim Donovan had gone into hiding—but he shot past. He swung the roadster past a bend; he eased off the pavement. Running close to a stone wall, over rough ground, he clicked off the lights and the ignition. Sitting tensely, listening again, he heard the sounds of the search continue from the darkness of the Kalmar estate.

"Stick close, Di!" He gripped the girl's arm as they climbed over the wall; they dropped to smooth ground beyond, and ducked into the shadow. As they hurried, a movement stirred the gloom ahead—Tim Donovan. The boy ran close; they paused together. Peering across the road, through the fence which enclosed the grounds, they watched the blinking of the flashlights in the depths of the gardens.

"Jimmy—I saw somebody get out of the house through a window!" the Irish lad exclaimed. "Just a few minutes ago—before you came out. I couldn't see his face, but—he acted like

67

a wild man, Jimmy! He ran like an animal—sometimes on all fours, sometimes with his arms swinging—and disappeared back there in the gardens."

Footfalls sounded near the gate of the Kalmar grounds. Out of the gloom, two men appeared with startling suddenness—men garbed in white. They wore the uniforms of hospital interns; they hurried to the gate and swung it shut. As they turned away, metal glinted in their hands—heavy revolvers. They broke suddenly into a run, turning back toward the house, as a hoarse shout sounded in the darkness.

"We've got him!"

"Hold that man!"

Near the house there was a frantic threshing in the bushes. A struggle was taking place. Quick-moving men shifted into a beam of light shafting from one of the windows. Others crowded toward them, reaching to grip the arms of a captive being dragged into the open. Five leaped upon the prisoner, fighting to restrain him, throwing their weight upon him. They forced him to the ground, pinioning his arms and legs; behind them appeared Dr. Kalmar, breathless.

"Be careful! He's strong as a gorilla! Take him in! Put him in the straight-jacket!"

Operator 5, sheltered behind the stone wall, watched intently as the prisoner was jerked up. The other men in white crowded beside the fugitive, still pinioning his arms, as they forced him toward the rear of the house. Snarling noises, like the savage protests of a trapped animal, tore from his throat. They pulled him out of sight behind the house; the slam of a door shut away his inarticulate cry of defiance.

Jimmy Christopher's fingers reached to the golden charm on his watch-chain. Quietly he said: "Tim, stay here. If Dr. Kalmar comes out before I return, you're to follow him, using the roadster. If he doesn't—watch sharp!"

"Jimmy—be careful!"

OPERATOR 5 smiled tightly as he vaulted the wall. He darted into the shadow of the hedge on the opposite side; he skirted along it noiselessly. When he reached the corner, he paused alertly, sensing a presence behind him. He turned; he saw a dark figure hastily following him. He pressed back a startled exclamation as Diane Elliot came to a breathless stop.

"Di—stay back!"

"If its not too dangerous for you, Jimmy Christopher," Diane retorted with a lift of her chin, "it's not too dangerous for me. Go right ahead—I'm following."

Jimmy Christopher knew that argument was useless. He gestured his anxious resignation and a chuckle came from the girl. Again he moved quietly along the fence, toward the rear of the estate; the girl followed at his heels. They passed beyond the house; they came to the brink of a raw earthen bank which made further progress impossible. The ground dropped away in a sheer cliff for fifty feet to the rocky bottom of a ravine; beyond it the iron fence ended.

"Going over," Jimmy Christopher said quietly. "You can't make it, Di."

"I'll make it all right, Jimmy! You watch!"

Operator 5 felt anxiety tighten his heart—concern for this plucky girl—yet he knew he could not restrain her. He gripped the fence; he swung himself up. Balancing, he seized Diane's hand and raised her. She dangled silken legs before she dropped into Operator 5's arms. They stood side by side, inside the fence, gazing across the gloomy grounds, at the shining windows, and listened into the brooding silence.

Jimmy Christopher moved from shadow to shadow with the girl, each maneuver carrying them closer to the house. He searched the darkness for a possible sentry; they sprang across an open space and over a plot of garden; they came to a pause at the wall of the house. Listening again, they heard the same strange muttering they had heard before—throaty voices, rising and falling as if with unrestrained, barbaric emotion—voices blending into a mumble that might have been issuing from the lips of jungle savages.

Operator 5's hand sought Diane Elliot's. His words were a whisper. "Di, in case we're spotted, you're to get back to the car

TIM DONOVAN

as soon as possible. Don't wait for me. Report as soon as possible to Z-7. Do you understand?"

The girl was peering into the darkness, listening to the throaty muttering; her eyes were widened with apprehension. "Yes, Jimmy! I'll—"

A shriek cut into Diane's words—a high-pitched cry of terror. It rang within the ivy-covered walls, mingled with a scuffling of feet. It was an animal scream that faded into a prolonged, piteous wail.

Operator 5 stiffened when he heard it, and as it faded into the continued muttering, he moved cautiously along the wall behind the garden plot.

Diane Elliot crept after him to a window. Stout iron bars criss-crossed it, anchored by heavy bolts. Behind the panes, a black drape hung. A mere slit of light shone at one side of the curtain. Jimmy Christopher leaned forward tensely, peering into the space beyond, from which the savage mumbling came....

THE ROOM was long, brilliantly lighted. Down its center ran an open aisle formed by two walls of iron bars reaching from floor to ceiling. The space behind each section was divided by other partitions of strong iron rods. Each cubicle space was a cell containing a cot. In each cell, a man was imprisoned behind a bolted door. There were twelve cells, twelve men....

From the lips of the prisoners, the chant of lament was issuing. Their eyes stared. Their hands moved restlessly from bar to bar. They swayed from position to position, like wild animals baffled by the walls of iron. Ceaselessly they shifted back and forth, the endless barbaric muttering coming continually from their loose lips....

Operator 5 peered at them. He drew back with lips hard-pressed. He whispered: "Madmen!"

Footfalls resounding in the room stilled the mumble. Jimmy Christopher turned back to the slit of light. A door at the far end of the corridor between the walls of bars had opened, and Dr. Anton Kalmar strode into the room quickly. Behind him, two men appeared, each garbed in white, holding a captive between them. The prisoner's face was contorted with frenzy; he was struggling against the tightness of the garment that bound his arms around his thick body. His eyes shone with insane ferocity as he strove to tear himself out of the binding straight-jacket....

Dr. Kalmar paused at one of the cells. He inserted a heavy key in the lock of its door. He stepped back and his voice rang: "Come out! Number Six, come out! Come quietly. Obey me!"

The prisoner called Number Six cowed before the commanding tone of the scientist. He shuffled forward from the cell in abject fear. He stood aside, his eyes fixed on the doctor's narrow face, his nostrils quivering, as the two assistants thrust the straight-jacketed prisoner into the vacated cell. The heavy iron door clanked shut; the bolt of the lock rasped into its socket. Furiously the prisoner flung himself against the bars, shrieking in anguish. Dr. Kalmar ignored him and turned to Number Six.

"Hear me! He betrayed his trust! You will take his place. You will obey me implicitly. If you do not, you will be destroyed. Do you understand—destroyed!"

Destroyed!

The word rang sharply in Operator 5's mind. He gazed intently at the pallid face of Dr. Kalmar as Number Six made an awkward gesture of obeisance. The scientist turned; Number Six shuffled after him with the docility of a beaten dog. They strode from the room. The two assistants followed and closed the door. Again Number Three shrieked in insane wrath; again the hysterical babble broke from the lax lips of the madmen in the cells.

Operator 5 stepped back. Diane Elliot glided after him through the shadows, toward the rear of the house. There they paused and listened while Jimmy Christopher searched the grounds with darkening eyes.

He said quietly: "There are no sentinels here. I'm going to try to get into the house. Diane—for God's sake, go back!"

"No, Jimmy! I won't leave you here alone!"

"Diane!" Operator 5 seized the girl's arms tightly. "Go back to the car! The sending unit of the short-wave transmitter in the roadster is tuned to the wavelength of headquarters B-3. Use it! Ask Z-7 to bring every available man here at once. They may arrive too late, but we've got to take the chance. Now, Di!"

Diane Elliot was trembling, peering deep into Operator 5's dark eyes. "All right, Jimmy. I'll go. But—you've got to be careful!"

HE WATCHED her move quietly through the darkness toward the fence. As she melted into the gloom, he approached another window at the rear corner of the house. Faint voices were sounding through it—the tones of Dr. Kalmar. The scientist's words, far-away but clear, reached Jimmy Christopher's ears as he paused and listened:

"That young man who was here—he is Operator 5 of the United States Intelligence. He is probably the most dangerous enemy we have. If I had thought he suspected me, I would never have allowed him to leave this house alive. But in the excitement—while Number Three tried to escape—I didn't have time to question him properly."

Grimly Jimmy Christopher listened.

"We cannot remain here longer—but that is of no importance. I am prepared to abandon everything in this house. It is a small loss compared to the priceless prize that is within our grasp. Now, immediately, we must go. Remember—more important than any other threat against us is the danger of Operator 5. We must find him and destroy him—destroy him so that his resurrection is utterly impossible!

"Get ready!"

Coldness crept around Jimmy Christopher's heart. He left the window. Step by step he approached a rear door sheltered by a small vine-covered porch. He eased upon the step, his hand slipping to his armpit holster—and suddenly he paused.

Inside the house, a bell began clanging. The sudden, metallic clamor sounded shrill in the night. Instantly, alarmed voices called within the house and heavy footfalls tramped. "The rear door!"

Operator 5 jerked back in consternation. A faint gleam of light caught his eye near one post of the porch. It was a vague round spot—an illuminated lens in a black box affixed to the upright. Jimmy Christopher glanced in the opposite direction and saw that the narrow beam from the lens was falling upon another crystal in a similar box fastened to a second post. The reason for the abrupt, startling alarm was revealed.

Operator 5, moving across the step, had unwittingly interrupted that invisible light-beam. The break had reacted upon a photo-electric cell. A relay had closed a contact, activating the bell inside the house. No human sentries were stationed upon the grounds, but the entrances to the mansion were guarded by these electric, ever-vigilant eyes. Now, answering the clamor of the gong men were rushing toward the door!

Jimmy Christopher whirled away. He began a swift run across the grounds. He realized that he was out-numbered, that the high fence constituted a trap. He peered around swiftly as he sprinted, attempting to locate Diane Elliot in the gloom, but he caught no glimpse of her. He sped toward the open space at the rear of the grounds as the doors of the house were flung open, as men came crowding out.

Suddenly—light! Giant globes sprang into brilliance along the fence. Their blinding shine flooded the grounds. The shadows were wiped away and with them all possible hiding-places vanished. At the same instant, a shaft of even whiter brilliance shot from the top of the house. On the roof, the giant eye of a searchlight opened, and the dazzling beam swung low across the grounds.

JIMMY CHRISTOPHER sprang aside wildly to escape it—but there was no shelter. Whirling, automatic in hand, he glimpsed a movement near the fence. Diane! She was gripping the bars, pulling herself up—and the shaft of the searchlight struck full upon her. Her face shone white in the glare; she dropped back frantically. Toward her, from the house, men were running. Jimmy Christopher swerved toward her and shouted: "Over, Di! Get over!"

His rush was blocked by two men who whirled in his way. He darted aside, springing back toward the brink of the ravine that cut off the rear of the grounds. Two sharp shots sounded. Operator 5 skirted along the raw edge of earth, hoping to reach the fence—but again white-clad men, guns in hand, darted to block his way. He brought up short, staring past them at the two other men who had closed in upon Diane Elliot, who were dragging her away from the fence.

Operator 5 leveled his gun, grimly facing the grounds, empty blackness behind him. On three sides, he faced grim-faced men silhouetted against the glare. The blinding beam of the searchlight on the roof stabbed into his eyes. He shaded his face; his gun was a waving menace. He peered intently at a lean figure which stood in the open directly in front of him.

Dr. Anton Kalmar was gripping the butt of a strange weapon in his hand. Its flaring muzzle was leveled at Jimmy Christopher. Operator 5 grimly lined his gun at the scientist; his finger tightened on the trigger but did not squeeze. Dr. Kalmar was standing beyond range of the automatic. Any bullet Operator 5 fired would drop into the grass before it reached the scientist. Backed by empty night, cornered by the threatening guns of the interns, Operator 5 defenselessly faced the weird weapon in Dr. Kalmar's hand.

It lightninged uncanny power at Jimmy Christopher. A hollow report sounded. A blinding white flare flashed. Through the night, the strange force struck, engulfing Jimmy Christopher. A swift paralysis seized him. Once, in a paroxysm of shock, he pulled the trigger of his automatic and his bullet whined into empty air. One instant the world was a bursting globe of searing light. Then—Jimmy Christopher dropped. Senseless, he fell past the brink of the cliff, into the maw of the night....

CHAPTER 6
THE HEAD OF HORROR

RINGING REPORTS, carrying across the road, chilled Tim Donovan's heart. He clung to the stone wall that sheltered him; he peered with pulse throbbing into the glare radiating from Dr. Kalmar's grounds. Quickly he scrambled across the wall. He crouched, his breath beating hotly, as sudden darkness blanketed down over the house and the grounds.

"Jimmy!" he whispered anxiously. "Jimmy!"

He searched the gloom. He heard running footfalls, a sharp voice issuing orders. He paused in turmoil, and suddenly he whirled to dash along the road. He raced around the bend, across the rough ground on which Operator 5 had left the roadster. He scrambled into the seat and his chubby hand shot to the switch of the radio equipment.

A torturous age passed before the tubes heated, while the Irish lad fitted 'phones to his ears and brought a microphone close to his lips. When a hiss sounded, signifying that the transmitter was operating, he checked the setting of the oscillator and blurted into the microphone:

"Calling B-3! Calling B-3!"

Silence…. Tim Donovan squirmed in agony. He painstakingly reset the dials. He strove to penetrate the background crackle of static. His voice took on a sharper edge.

"Calling B-3! B-3!"

Suddenly an answer came. "B-3! Got you! Go ahead!"

A sob burst from the boy's lips. "Tim Donovan calling! Oper-

78

ator 5 and Diane Elliot—in Dr. Kalmar's house. Z-7 knows the address! Send men! Send every man you can! Emergency!"

"I'll relay your message to Z-7 at once! Hello, Tim Donovan! Hello!"

No answer came from the roadster's short-wave transmitter. The frantic lad had jerked off the 'phones and dropped the microphone. He squirmed out of the car and darted across the road. He flung himself through the gloom along the fence, peering through the bars to search the grounds. Now thick darkness lay over the house, over the spreading lawn. Darkness and silence….

The silence continued until a muffled throbbing sounded in the distance. Tim Donovan identified it as the rushing exhausts of motors; but he could not place it. He hurried along the fence and called Jimmy Christopher's name. He brought up short at the brink of the cliff, recoiling from the threatening depths of the darkness looked below. Baffled, he started to turn back—and paused.

A faint rustle—a noise so vague that it might have been the stirring of dry leaves in the night wind—stopped him. Almost inaudible, it came again—from the thick darkness of the ravine. Tim Donovan's small hands clenched into determined fists. He hurried to the fence; he dropped flat. Gripping the iron rods, he slid himself down, over the crumbling edge of earth—and dangled.

He dragged himself back, anxiously, striving to find a foothold in the earth. His body strained as he swung himself, hooking his heels on the soft edge. Swiftly shifting his hands, he pulled himself forward. Panting, he brought himself up. He skirted along the edge, alertly watching the darkness of the grounds, listening into the silence.

Again—that faint rustle! Tim Donovan stopped short. "Jimmy!" he called in a burst of breath. He peered over the bank; he glimpsed a vague, dark shape against the black wall of earth. Springing ahead, he dropped flat, head and shoulders thrust out into space, peering again at the baffling shape below. It moved slightly, and with the movement came another riffle of leaves.

"Jimmy!"

IN THE gloom, Tim Donovan discerned Operator 5 sprawling against the

Lying in the shallow tray was the head of secret agent R-4!

steeply sloping bank. Jimmy Christopher was toeing into it, clinging with both hands to a clump of bushes. Dislodged dirt spilled upon him as the roots yielded from the soft earth. Bit by bit, the bushes were tearing out…. Tim Donovan frantically reached down. His small hands closed firmly about Jimmy Christopher's wrist

A breathy warning sounded below: "Tim! Get back, boy! I'll pull you down with me!"

"I've got you, Jimmy! Dig in! You can get up! You can get up!"

Every muscle in the tough lad's body strained as he strove to lift Operator 5. Dirt spilled down again. Quick breathing sounded below. Tim Donovan wriggled back, his breath beating hotly, his fingers aching with the strain of his grip. Inch by inch, he braced himself farther from the edge. Jimmy Christopher's hands rose beyond the brink. They found fresh holds. With a renewed, straining effort, the boy shifted position, dug in his heels, pulled with all his strength.

Operator 5 rolled upon the edge of the cliff. He jerked himself up breathlessly. Tim Donovan clung to his hand, peering into his face with tear-filled eyes.

Jimmy Christopher's lips curved with a grim smile, his arm tightened across Tim Donovan's shoulders: "Thanks, Tim—thanks, old-timer! I would have dropped in another minute!"

"Gee, Jimmy! Are you all right?"

"Diane, Tim!" Operator 5 interrupted quickly. "Have you seen her?"

"No!"

Operator 5 straightened, his dark eyes searching the grounds, alertly listening. He brought his electric torch from his pocket; he turned its beam downward past the edge of the cliff. Below, at the base of the steep wall, jagged rocks lay, their sharp edges gleaming in the beam. Grimly, Operator 5 swung the light up and backed away.

"They left me for dead. The doctor used the new magnesium gun, Tim.* We've got to find Di!"

"Jimmy—look!"

Tim Donovan pointed breathlessly toward the windows at the side of the house. Behind the panes, a sudden flare of light appeared—naked flames climbing up the drapes. As the fabric vanished in the mounting tongues of fire, the rooms beyond became visible—rooms filled with crimson light. The gleam reflected in Jimmy Christopher's narrowed eyes as he started forward.

"Stick close, Tim!"

He ran to the rear door of the house. Deliberately, when he reached the porch, he interrupted the photo-electric light-beam. Instantly the bell inside the house resumed its clamor; but its alarm brought no response. No voices rose; no footfalls

---

* AUTHOR'S NOTE: The existence of a new weapon was revealed recently in the *New York Times*. It is a pistol, resembling in appearance somewhat an automobile headlight without the lens, capable of firing magnesium charges which can stun men and animals a mile away. The patent on this new weapon is held by a German inventor who was forced to flee from his native land. It was demonstrated recently in Paris.

sounded. Operator 5 seized the knob of the door and demanded breathlessly:

"Did you see them leave, Tim? Did they go out the gate?"

"No, Jimmy!"

OPERATOR 5 pushed into an elaborately outfitted kitchen. He hurried through it, along a corridor. He thrust open a door and saw, beyond it, the iron-barred cages. Now each cell-door was standing open. Now the fortified spaces were empty. The madmen had vanished....

Operator 5 turned quickly and opened a door at the opposite side of the corridor. The air was thick with smoke; the sharp pungency stung his lungs and eyes. He turned sharply to order Tim Donovan: "Find a telephone! Report the fire! Make it fast—the whole house is going!"

The boy sprinted along the hall as Operator 5 opened the doorway. Cold air gusted up, carrying musty dampness. He snapped a light-switch and ran down a flight of cement steps. The vast space beneath the house was crowded with packing cases. In one wall stood a broad iron door, open; beyond it glistened the earthen walls of a tunnel.

Jimmy Christopher slid into the passage, his flashlight in his hand. He darted along it, noting fresh footprints in the damp floor. The tunnel curved. For a long way, Operator 5 followed it, and a fresh flow of air rushed past him. He approached an opening. The passage ended abruptly, screened by a high, thick hedge.

Jimmy Christopher shouldered into the open night. His torch flicked across a field. Nearby, two grassless ruts testified that automobiles had frequently come and gone from this spot.

It was sheltered from the road; it was silent. The beam of Jimmy Christopher's light, playing upon the ground, disclosed the tracks of tires—fresh.

This way Dr. Kalmar and his assistants and his madmen had fled. And Diane—?

Operator 5 plunged back through the hedge and hurried along the tunnel. When he reached the cellar, he bounded up the stairs into thicker smoke. The fire was roaring beyond open doors, spreading across the carpets, enveloping the furniture. The black, blinding fumes testified that oil had been spread—fuel to hasten the blaze. Jimmy Christopher sped along the corridor, thrust open another door, and looked into a white-walled operating room agleam with cabinets, surgical implements and sterilizers—at glass and enamel twinkling through a thickening vapor.

He turned away as Tim Donovan, face beaded with sweat, hurried from the fume-filled library. "The call's through!"

Again Operator 5 thrust open a door. On the sill he paused. The air inside was misted, though a lack of inflammable material had not spread the fire far here. It was a huge, elaborate laboratory, filled with strange devices. In the center stood a contrivance like a tall see-saw, its leaves short and broad. Beyond, on benches, sat complicated pump arrangements. Striding in, Operator 5 turned toward a wall against which a high table was standing—and stopped short.

Horror froze him. On the table was placed a shallow dish. In the dish, an amber liquid glittered. Supported in the fluid on a wire rack sat—a human head!

THE HEAD of Secret Agent R-4! Rigid, frozen with fascination, Jimmy Christopher stood. He peered intently, hypnotically, at the human head in the tray. Its eyes were open! Its eyes were staring at him! The skin was fresh and life-like; the lips were drawn into a tight grimace. Severed from its body, the veins in the stump of a neck seeming to throb as if with life, the head of R-4 gazed at Jimmy Christopher!

Operator 5 stepped forward wide-eyed, chilled with the horror of the sight. Behind the head on the tray, an arrangement of complicated apparatus was functioning. The hum of a small motor penetrated the rising crackling of the flames in the other rooms. From a glass reservoir, half full of a fluid of the redness of blood, glass tubes sectioned with rubber led to the severed head. The mechanism of the motor was causing a pump to send throbbing impulses through the tubes with the regular beat of a human heart. A bellows was breathing. In unbounded amazement, Operator 5 stepped back again; an involuntary gasp broke from his lips as he gazed at the severed head.

Its eyes had turned!

Jimmy Christopher saw the gaze of the severed head shift—shift to Tim Donovan. The lids blinked. The lips trembled. The nostrils quivered. And again the eyeballs of the severed head shifted to Operator 5's face, eyes filled with a piteous gaze.

Tim Donovan blurted in amazement: "It's alive, Jimmy! That head's alive!"

"Yes," Jimmy Christopher assented. "And that's the horrible thing about it. If I take it away to bury with the rest of the body, I'll actually be killing R-4!" He looked at the severed head. "But

that's the only thing I can do! It's the only decent thing to do!"
He gazed at the object in the shallow dish. "Do you understand,
R-4?"

The eyes blinked again; the piteous look remained in them,
as if pleading for death. Operator 5 shuddered, snatched up a
white surgical gown, and wrapped the head up in it. Tim Donovan was wide-eyed with horror. He obeyed with alacrity when
Operator 5 choked: "Out, Tim! Quick!"

Thicker fumes were gusting through the doors into the hallway. The air was unbreathable. Withering heat blasted from the
rising flames. Jimmy Christopher thrust the Irish lad ahead of
him. They groped blindly toward the last door and hurried into
the kitchen. They thrust out the rear entrance, into clearer air,
and spun about to see snarling sheets of flame whipping up the
sides of the house.

They hurried together to the gate and through it. They darted
to the roadster as the sound of sirens sang out of the distance.
Unmoving they watched while fire-engines streaked down the
road and through the gate. They saw streams of white-hiss-
ing water play out of the hose-nozzles as rubber-coated men
swarmed to fight the fire. Higher and higher the flames reached,
lighting the zenith….

Lips pinched, eyes darkened and glittering with the light of
the blaze, Operator 5 stood motionless. Tim Donovan's wide
eyes searched his face. His voice was strained, ringing, when
he said:

"Dr. Kalmar must have taken Di with him, Tim! They've
got Di!"

Over the road, bright headlights glimmered. A string of cars came rushing toward the flaming house. Operator 5 kept out of sight until they stopped near the fence, until he saw the familiar faces of the men—who alighted from them. He hurried forward, with Tim Donovan at his side, toward the gray-clad figure of Z-7.

"Chief!" Z-7 whipped about. "It's no use, Chief—that house is doomed. Kalmar and his men fired it and fled. They're traveling in cars—we've got to find them at once! They've got Di, Chief! God knows what that human fiend will use her for!"

"Kalmar!" Z-7 exclaimed. "Then you believe—!"

"I've got absolute proof," Operator 5 said, motioning to the white bundle he carried. "But Di! They left from the field beyond the house. The tracks are plain. Get your men after them and broadcast the alarm. We've got to find Di, Chief! We've got to find her!"

Z-7 shouted crisp commands. Jimmy Christopher hurried to his roadster. Tim scrambled in beside him as he spurted ahead to lead the way. As he passed the gate of the Kalmar estate, Z-7 heard his grim words:

"Nothing can save it! Thank God nothing can save that house where the dead were made to live again!"

CHAPTER 7
VIGIL BY AIR

THE HUSH of early morning lay over New York City. The myriad lights of the metropolis were dimmed. The hum of the streets had vanished into the darkness. The city slept while, unseen and scarcely heard, a man-made bat hovered over it in the night.

Above the building in which Loft C of the United States Intelligence Service was located, its vanes whirling, its motor muffled, an autogyro circled slowly. Operator 5's suggestion and Z-7's order had taken it into the sky above the quiet canyons of the city. At its controls, an expert pilot sat alert, jockeying it steadily above his position. In its rear cubby, a man perched with night binoculars searching the air around him. It was Intelligence Operator H-8; his was a gambling vigil.

For hours the craft had hovered in the air, sometimes dropping, sometimes climbing, always slowly circling. Its fuel was running low. The hour was approaching when the second gyro ordered to this detail would relieve it. Constantly, the pilot plied the controls; constantly, H-8 probed into the dark air with his lenses. Long minute ticked away after long minute....

Abruptly H-8 tightened. The sweep of his glasses caught a faint, glistening flutter in the air. He steadied; he sought to find the dark sparkle again. He went breathless when he glimpsed it—a fast movement across the chasms of the city—a winged thing speeding through the faint light, toward the building that lay below.

A carrier pigeon! One of the birds stolen by the wearers of the golden crown! Painstakingly, H-8 followed its swift flight as it fluttered down, circling. He slapped the shoulder of his pilot and pointed in the direction from which the bird had appeared. The huge bat swerved off swiftly, darting in a straight line, until its position lay directly south of the building. There it slowed and hovered again.

H-8 peered at the lighted window of Loft C through his glasses and saw the pigeon wafting through. Inside the rear room—freed now of the Death Dew that the first bird had carried—an Intelligence agent appeared. He caught the pigeon. He turned away; H-8's last glimpse was of his hand detaching a message tube from the returned bird's leg.

Again H-8 settled down to his wearing vigil, determined never to relax for a moment until the second gyro appeared to spell him…. Far below, tiny cars crawled. To the West flowed the dark band of the Hudson. Across that ribbon the lights of ferries occasionally sparkled. Along the waterfront, darkness lay thick.

Toward a gloomy building in the Battery, a sleek roadster turned. Operator 5 swung it to the curb, stepped out and waited while another drew up behind him and Z-7 alighted. Grim-faced, worn, they trod to the entrance of the gray-stone structure. They knocked upon its heavy, locked door. A latch clicked, and a man in the uniform of a Customs Inspector admitted them with a cordial greeting.

Operator 5 strode into a partitioned office. Anxiously he called the number of headquarters B-3; quickly he exchanged signals. He demanded connection with the chief-dispatcher and asked tightly: "Have the men who were sent to Kalmar's place reported? Is there any news of Diane Elliot?"

"Most of the reports have come in, Operator 5," the dispatcher answered. "None of the cars has been located. There is no clue to Miss Elliot's whereabouts. I'm sorry, but—we're doing our utmost."

Jimmy Christopher's eyes darkened haggardly as he lowered the phone. "God, Chief!" he exclaimed huskily. "We've got to find Di! We've got to find her!"

Z-7 SCOWLED angrily. "If there is anything we can do that we have not already done—"

Operator 5's shoulders squared. "Our only hope is to locate Dr. Kalmar. It's a sure thing that he has many headquarters. He may be in the city now—he may be hundreds of miles from here. Our best lead—" Jimmy Christopher turned grimly to the Customs Inspector. "We are here to view the body shipped on the S.S. *Ultima* this evening."

"I've been holding it for you—though no one has appeared so far to claim it."

The Inspector conducted them out of the office, into the vast storage space beyond. In the cavernous room sat piles of cases, bins of bundles—shipments held for payment of customs duty, seized under suspicious circumstances. Toward a huge, long case—shaped like a casket built for a giant—the Inspector led the way.

Operator 5 inspected its markings. They declared that the box contained a work of art, that it had been dispatched from Wescar, the capitol of Dalgary, a small Balkan nation. Its address was *The Winship Galleries,* on Madison Avenue, New York. Iron bands had been loosened from it, and the lid raised. Operator 5 peered inside and saw that the box was lined with cork and packed with lumps of white from which fumes rose slowly.

"Solid carbon dioxide," Jimmy Christopher mused. "Dry ice. Chosen because of its low temperature—109 degrees below zero—and because it melts into a gas instead of a liquid."

The metal coffin inside was unmarked. Its clamps had been loosened. Operator 5 gripped the edge of the headpiece and lifted it. He gazed upon the placid, white face of a corpse. His eyes narrowed: he stepped back and his alarmed gaze shot to Z-7's eyes.

"Chief! That is the body of a man whose name is known around the world!"

"What?"

"A little more than a week ago, the news of his death was cabled to this country. He died of heart-failure. His death constituted a minor crisis in Balkan affairs of state. That man is Chancellor Ulreck of Dalgary!"

Z-7 blurted: "Good God! It's not possible!"

"It is Ulreck!" Jimmy Christopher insisted, turning sharply to the Inspector. "That casket must be re-sealed. The box must be closed and the bands replaced so that it appears not to have been opened. When it is called for, you are to allow it to be taken in spite of all irregularities."

Jimmy Christopher turned. "One of our best men is to be put on the job of watching this box, Chief. He is never to take his eyes off it. When it is claimed, he is to follow it to its destination—which will not be the address on the box. This body is one of the few chances we have of reaching Dr. Kalmar—of finding his new hideaway."

Z-7 strode into the office. Operator 5 waited, absorbed in

thought, while the chief talked over the telephone with head-quarters B-3. The Inspector was already laboring to restore the original condition of the box. When the Washington chief returned, he and Operator 5 left the Customs house and reentered the Diesel-engined roadster.

JIMMY CHRISTOPHER drove northward rapidly. The thick darkness that precedes dawn blanketed the city when he drew to a stop at the entrance of the famed Vertex Building. With Z-7, he ascended in the elevator; he strode at once into the inner offices of headquarters B-3. Immediately he summoned the chief-dispatcher and asked: "I want news of Miss Elliot! Have the reports—?"

"All reports are in, sir! There is no news of her. We are absolutely unable to locate her!"

Grim-faced, Jimmy Christopher lifted the telephone from Z-7's desk. He called Address Y. Tim's eager voice responded at once.

"Tim! No word from Di?"

"No! What can we do, Jimmy?"

Operator 5 lowered the telephone to find Z-7 peering at him. The chief's gaze was grim.

The shrill ring of the telephone trilled; immediately the door of the communications-room snapped open. Through the clatter of teletype machines, the chief-dispatcher called in: "Loft C on the wire, Chief! Urgent!"

Z-7 quickly took up the telephone. Operator 5 shifted to an extension instrument which would enable him to listen in on the conversation. He heard the deep voice of the secret agent on the other end of the line: "Chief, a second carrier pigeon flew in a short while ago. It brought a message addressed to Operator 5."

Z-7 ordered: "Read it! Now!"

"This is the message, chief. 'To Operator 5. You are my most dangerous enemy. You shall not hinder me. Withdraw from this case at once. Unless you assure me by your actions within twenty-four hours that you have abandoned your purpose, I shall send you evidence that the girl you love has become *Yajna!* Signed, The Master of Death'."

OPERATOR 5'S hand whitened on the telephone as Z-7 snapped: "Send that message to headquarters at once! The men in the gyros must stay on the job—"

"They've checked the bird's direction. They're ready to trace it still farther if another bird appears!"

"Good!" Z-7 racked the telephone. Jimmy Christopher turned to face him haggardly. The chief took up reports that had been placed on his desk while Operator 5 studied a message that he had taken from the files. An exclamation came from the Washington chief.

"Our agents are gathering information hourly which proves the vast extent of the Master of Death's plan. Reports from Boston, Chicago, Philadelphia, Baltimore—a score of cities. Deaths by violence, and a little earthen image found at the scene of each one! The image you called Yama! Each bearing a number—"

Operator 5 listened intently.

"Here is an instance of a man shot through the brain, and the image found near him bore the numeral one. A body discovered decapitated—the number on the image is two. Another body, the heart cut out—and the number is three. God! What can it mean?"

"It means—" Operator 5 broke off abruptly. "Go ahead, Chief! Those other reports?"

"From almost every important city there are reports of vanishing bodies—of dead men and women disappearing mysteriously. In each case—"

"In each case, Chief," Operator 5 broke in, "the bodies vanished very quickly after death occurred—before they could be embalmed! Those corpses were intended for resurrection! The process of embalming would have made resurrection impossible. I warned you, Chief, that the Master of Death has a vast espionage system in operation—and probably each secret agent in it is himself a living dead man. Their duty is to locate and spirit away the bodies of the dead. The dead become living corpses, disciples of the Master of Death! It is impossible to say where these operations will stop, Chief. That same power may strike at the leaders of our industry—at the leaders of our government!"

Z-7's face had gone white. "I still can't believe—" he began, and broke off, peering at other reports on his desk. They were sheets to which photographs of fingerprints had been pasted, to which cards had been clipped. Z-7 jerked to his feet in unbounded amazement.

"Good God! These are the prints found at Loft C—left by the men who Murdered R-4! They are the fingerprints—every one—of *dead men!*"

Quietly Operator 5 declared: "It is as I expected, Chief!"

"Dead men!" Z-7 roared. "Living corpses went into that loft and killed R-4! There is no possible doubt of it—here are the records of the murderer's deaths, copied from the New York City files—legal proof that those men were dead!"

"**EVERY DAY,** Chief," Jimmy Christopher declared, "the army of the dead is growing. Unless we can stop the plan of the Master of Death, it will grow until it numbers thousands and millions—until the United States becomes a land of living dead who hail the Master of Death as their ruler, whose families worship at the shrine of a promised immortality. That is the danger we face!"

Z-7 peered appalled at Operator 5.

"Not only is the Master of Death wielding his power in this country, Chief—he is reaching abroad. The case of Chancellor Ulreck proves it. That body was brought here for the purpose of resurrecting it. A plan of the Master of Death went into operation the moment Ulreck died. Here is a report that substantiates my statement."

The Washington chief took the cabled information which Jimmy Christopher had drawn from the files. He read rapidly:

... WDC-13... STRANGE CIRCUMSTANCES SURROUNDING DEATH OF CHANCELLOR ULRECK... FUNERAL THIS MORNING BUT DEMONSTRATION FAR LESS THAN EXPECTED... FLAGS NOT FLYING AT HALF MAST... NONE OF ULRECK'S FAMILY AT FUNERAL... ULRECK'S CASKET SEEMED SUSPICIOUSLY LIGHT... ULRECK

FAMILY HAS EMBARKED SECRETLY FOR NEW YORK... HAD I NOT VIEWED ULRECK'S BODY THE BRIEF PERIOD IT LAY IN STATE I SHOULD SUSPECT THAT HE IS NOT DEAD... L-9, WD....

"That report means, Chief," Jimmy Christopher declared, "that Ulreck's family has been promised he will live again. They are somewhere in this country now, waiting for his resurrection!"

Z-7 sank into a chair, his head wagging. "I am still trying to grasp it all. How is it possible?"

"It's possible, all right," Jimmy Christopher declared. "Dr. Kalmar's laboratory was perfectly equipped for resurrecting the dead. I already knew of some of the devices. The teeter-board, for instance, which starts the blood flowing again in the dead body.* It was all there and all of it had been used to bring corpses

---

* Author's Note: Dr. Cornish, describing the method he would use if granted permission to resurrect an executed criminal, said:

"Using a gas mask, I would enter the lethal chamber and remove the corpse as quickly as possible. *Rigor mortis* does not begin in a human body for six or eight hours after actual death, whereas it attacks the body of a dog in about three hours. But time is precious in these experiments.

"To counteract the cyanide poisoning, I would inject methylene blue. I would start the heart by a combination of artificial respiration and injection of a fluid into a large artery under pressure. The injection would consist principally of human blood selected to 'match' that of the dead man and to it would be added herapin, an extract of liver, to prevent clotting.

"There would be also epinephrine in the fluid to constrict the small arteries of the body and make it easier to build up the blood-pressure to about 20

back to life. In addition, there was in that room a secret of Dr. Kalmar's amazing success. He has perfected the technique in some way by experiments on human beings."

"How can you be sure?"

"The madmen I saw in their cages were one proof that Dr. Kalmar has spent years perfecting his technique. He must have concentrated on the problem of nullifying the effects of death on the human brain.* That he has succeeded almost completely is testified by the existence of the man who called himself Karant, by the men who murdered R-4."

AGAIN Z-7 studied the photographs of the dead men's

inches of water pressure, which seems to be necessary to start the heart beating. The methylene blue would be kept separate from the mixture until the moment for starting the injection, otherwise it might damage the red corpuscles before it had time to become diluted by spreading through the body.

"We believe it is possible to perfect such a method, in which our efforts would benefit humanity."

* AUTHOR'S NOTE: One of the chief difficulties met by experimenters in resurrection has been the effect of the total stoppage of blood circulation on the brain. Dr. Cornish, having succeeded in reviving a dead dog, stated after the animal had remained in a coma for twelve days, "I am afraid that the dog will be an idiot the rest of his days."

One of the experimenters at the Mayo Clinic declared in this vein: "We found that in every case in which the circulation to the brain had been stopped for over seven minutes, the resuscitated animal never regained consciousness although some of them lived in coma. Until some very potent

fingerprints found at Loft C. He peered wordlessly as Operator 5 briskly continued:

"In every way, Dr. Kalmar's ghastly experiments have reached farther toward conquering death than any others ever performed. You are bewildered, Chief, because this is new to you—but I have examined scientific records and discovered that a vast store of knowledge lies behind Dr. Kalmar's successful experiments. All of it is scientifically proven, and the way was opened decades ago. When I told you of the living, severed head of R-4 in that laboratory, you stared your disbelief. But you saw the condition of that head, Chief—and the forerunners of that apparently miraculous experiment were performed years ago in Moscow by one of the pioneers in the study of resurrection." *

substance is discovered which will revive degenerated brain tissue, such procedures are of little practical use."

In his later experiments, however, Dr. Cornish found evidence that the brain of his experimental dog had not been damaged. The difficulty resolved itself into a matter of technique, which promised a definite solution.

* AUTHOR'S NOTE: These experiments, among the most amazing in medical history, were successfully performed by Professor Sergei Brjuchenenko, and his assistants, Drs. S.J. Tchechulin and C.I. Spaso-kukoysky, in Moscow. Dr. Brjuchenenko, the inventor of the artificial heart machine, tells the story in his own words in the German scientific weekly, *Die Umschau:*

"Two dogs were chloroformed. Into the bloodstream of one, Germanin (a preparation which prevents the coagulation of blood and which is administered in cases of sleeping sickness) was injected. Thereupon blood was drained from the animal and the lungs carefully isolated. The blood flowed into a reservoir of the apparatus, which is the equivalent of the heart. Lungs and machine were then connected. The machine was now ready to 'beat' and take the place of the natural heart."

The doctor then all but severed the head of the other dog from the trunk. The slightest slip of the knife would have made the success of the experiment impossible, since the natural heart could not at this time be allowed to stop for an instant. Finally the head of the dog was connected with the trunk only by four principal arteries and a few nerves. Still the head did not die. The doctor's account continues:

"Now came the critical moment. The head was ready to be completely severed and connected with the apparatus. We bent every effort to effect the transfer from the natural to the artificial circulatory system without interrupting life for a single moment. First we connected the tubes of the machine with a few blood-vessels in the head. We started the pump. The artificial heart began to beat. Blood started to circulate through the head and to assist the dog's own heart. Then we cut the remaining blood-vessels and connected with the machine."

The experimenters saw the blood coursing through the tubes of the artificial heart, red as it entered the head because it had been oxygenated in the artificial lung, dark blue as it flowed out. At first the severed head seemed to be in a deep sleep.

"After a lapse of twenty or thirty minutes pronounced signs of life began to appear. The eyes opened with characteristic living appearance. The head now responded to the weakest stimuli. The eyelids winked.... When the ear was pulled, it contracted muscularly as it would under more natural circumstances. In some experiments, the eyes closed when an electric light was brought near them." When the severed head was irritated, "We had to

Operator 5 turned quickly to a file and placed a thick folder in front of Z-7.

"There are my transcriptions of the medical records. We are dealing with cold, scientific facts. The devilish cunning of Dr. Kalmar shows itself in the way he has cloaked his scientific machines with mysticism. His teeter-boards and artificial hearts were not exposed to the congregation in the Temple of the Crown in Carbonville, Chief. He appealed to those people through a sense of religion—the craving for worship which lies deep in every human heart. That is the man's devilish shrewdness—that is the greatest danger!"

Z-7 sat tensely, listening to each ringing word of Operator 5.

"The Master of Death is granting to human beings, in actuality, what religion only vaguely promises. He promises, and he actually gives, a continued, certain life on this earth! People are flocking to him because he grants them release from the ghastly fear of death. His power will grow swiftly—it will wipe away

---

hold the head on the plate with our hands" in order to keep the tubes from being torn away. "The muzzle opened wide, the teeth were stripped as if there were every intention of biting or barking."

Most remarkable of all, pieces of sausage or cheese were actually devoured, to be ejected by the open neck. In a word, the isolated head behaved exactly as if it were still attached but under anesthesia. It was possible to keep it alive in this fashion for three and a half hours."

Dr. Brjuchenenko further declared: "There can be no question that in its initial stages death is only apparent. Only later does it actually occur."

These experiments were begun as far back as the 1890s.

all religions as we know them. It will elevate Dr. Kalmar to a position more despotic than that of any other living being. He is immortal—and he possesses the power to rule the world!"

"Do you mean," Z-7 demanded in a husky tone, "that this human devil actually plans to place himself in such a position?"

"He does! Be certain of that. Every move betrays his purpose. He has already built up a ritual—a quasi-religious procedure, to accompany his resurrections. It has a double purpose. It strengthens the worship of his followers, and it destroys those who oppose him. His double-edged sword is—human sacrifice!

"Hamilton Wharton was such a sacrifice. The men whose destruction is told in your reports have been sacrifices to the same Vedic Hindu gods! They are called *Yajna*. From them, as they die, the Master of Death appears to snatch their souls, and he gives those souls to the dead who are about to live again!"

"But a civilized people will not flock to such barbarianism!" Z-7 objected. "They will not believe in this transfer of souls!"

"Millions in the Orient already believe in it, Chief. Thousands of our own people are embracing that belief. I have seen it grip hundreds, who gloried in the murder of a man because it apparently released his soul to the use of the dead. If that spirit sweeps the United States, Chief—if our millions turn to the worship of the Master of Death who grants them eternal life—the United States is doomed!"

Z-7 DEMANDED tensely: "How can we possibly fight that man? If death cannot destroy him—?"

"Death cannot destroy his power, Chief. Should Dr. Kalmar suffer what we term 'natural death' his assistants surely stand ready to resurrect him with his own devices, his own secret. It can be repeated again and again. And even if it could not—even if complete destruction should wipe Dr. Kalmar out of existence—his assistants will be able to carry on. The people will worship them as they now worship him."

"In God's name, what can we do?" the Washington chief insisted.

"There is only one possible way to destroy the Master of Death. That is to show that Dr. Kalmar himself, and his assistants, possess no divine power—that instead they make use of reliable scientific devices which any trained technician can use. We cannot destroy the great discovery he has made, but we can change the use to which he has put it."

Z-7 studied Operator 5's white face intently. "A plan is forming in your mind! You are perfecting a strategy!"

Jimmy Christopher nodded slowly. "Yes, Chief—but it is a slim chance. It needs the perfect opportunity. Perhaps we will be able to make that opportunity for ourselves. But, until we can reach Dr. Kalmar, we are helpless."

Jimmy Christopher turned quickly to the telephone. He consulted a directory and quickly put through a call. He spoke quietly into the instrument when a voice he knew responded.

"F-4!" he exclaimed. "You're watching the body that was taken from the *Ultima* this evening? Have any arrangements yet been made—?"

"There has been no move made to claim it," the operator at the Customs house answered. "I'll report at the first development"

Operator 5 pronged the receiver. Z-7 was peering at him intently. The Washington chief said quietly, "I realize your position only too well. God knows we need you on this case. But if you wish to withdraw, for Diane's sake—if you wish to protect her by—"

Jimmy Christopher interrupted by again lifting the receiver. He called Address Y again. Tim Donovan answered. "Tim! Haven't you heard from Diane?"

"No, Jimmy, nothing!"

Jimmy Christopher's face was white as he confronted Z-7. His fingers strayed slowly to the little golden death's head on his watch-charm. "I am not abandoning this case, Chief," he said levelly. "Diane would want me to see it through—and I will! But, God! We can only but wait—wait—*wait!*"

CHAPTER 8
TEMPLE OF IMMORTALS

T HE LIGHT of the next afternoon was fading when Operator 5 entered John Christopher's home. Wearily, he trudged up the stairs. Tim Donovan hurried toward him as he strode into the living-room; the boy peered anxiously into his dark-lined face. A sleepless night, a wearing, day-long vigil had made Jimmy Christopher's face haggard, but his eyes gleamed with a hard, undiminished brightness.

"Jimmy!" Tim Donovan exclaimed. "No word yet?"

"No word, Tim," Operator 5 answered slowly. He turned to

grip his father's hand, and a faint smile tightened his lips. "We are doing everything possible, Dad, but—"

Ex-Operator Q-6 asked quickly. "But is there any real danger for Di, Jimmy? If Dr. Kalmar is able to revive the dead—if other men are in possession of his technique—?"

"Dr. Kalmar is able to revive the dead *when he pleases,*" Operator 5 pointed out grimly. "He possesses a secret which no other scientists now possess. Diane will surely be sacrificed in the unholy ritual of the Master of Death, if—"

John Christopher cut in gravely: "I understand, my boy. I am deeply concerned for Di. Yet I am anxious that Dr. Kalmar's secret should not be lost. It is the most vital scientific discovery of the ages. Since learning of it, I have felt a new hope, a new lift of the spirit. I am losing my fear of death!"

Operator 5 examined his father's shining face intently. "Dr. Kalmar," he declared coldly, "is a merciless murderer. He is less a scientist than a man obsessed with a cruel ambition for power. We cannot even guess how far he has gone. He has sought sacrifices everywhere—he has found them. Every mysterious killing hints of the intrigue of that human devil. Remember that, Dad! Never forget it!"

"I know, my boy," Operator 5's father said gravely. "I know. Yet—"

John Christopher's voice faded; he stood self-absorbed, his eyes shining with a strange light, as Operator 5 took up the telephone. Jimmy Christopher called headquarters B-3 and exchanged signals. Z-7's voice rang over the wire.

"No report yet, Chief, concerning Ulreck's body?"

"None, my boy! No move has been made to claim it. Perhaps Dr. Kalmar suspects we have learned of it.... I have another report here—a message from Loft C. A third carrier pigeon has returned, carrying a message. It is signed by the Master of Death and addressed to you!"

"What message, Chief?" Operator 5 demanded grimly.

"It reads: Most of the twenty-four hours has already elapsed. At midnight tonight, you will have abandoned your case, or the girl you love will be destroyed and you will face destruction with her. Heed my warning!"

Operator 5's lips curved coldly. "I still have a few hours, Chief—and I intend to use them!"

Z-7 answered solemnly: "Very well! Our men in the autogyros have again shifted their position in attempting to trail the carrier pigeons. They have moved south. They are over the Battery now. It seems incredible that the birds could have been taken unnoticed to one of the big office buildings there. It may be that the pigeons are being liberated from a boat in the harbor."

"The first was released by someone who was watching the loft, Chief, but the others were carried farther away! Order that patrol maintained every minute, day and night. We must be ready to act—"

JIMMY CHRISTOPHER left the telephone while Tim Donovan watched him anxiously. He sank exhaustedly into a chair and the boy perched on its arm. Operator 5 sighed profoundly.

"God! It's the most diabolical plan! Most of those who die are possible subjects for resurrection—all the victims of heart diseases, shock, hemorrhage, asphyxiation, drowning. The families of the resurrected and their friends, are certain to become devoted worshipers of the Master of Death. There is nothing he cannot achieve if backed by the unquestioning will of the people. The destruction of the United States—the rule of the entire world!"

Tim Donovan had been thinking seriously. Now he spoke quietly. "Jimmy, show me a new trick, will you?"

Operator 5 smiled wanly. "Certainly, Tim. I've got a new one that will keep you guessing. Wait here, old-timer."

He rose wearily and strode into the work-rooms at the rear of the house—rooms crowded with strange appliances of his own devising—where he conducted researches in chemistry and radio transmission, where he originated and perfected the feats of legerdemain which Tim Donovan delighted to see. He returned to the living-room almost at once, bringing with him a large bandanna handkerchief, folded in one hand.

"Now Dad's hat, Tim," he requested. The boy brought it Operator 5 placed the hat brim upward on the table. Tim stood back, watching intently as Jimmy Christopher took the handkerchief by two corners, shook it out and held it before him.

"You see, Tim," he said, turning the bandanna about so that both sides were visible in turn, "there is nothing suspicious about it. Yet it possesses magical powers. Now, watch very carefully and you'll see an amazing sight."

Jimmy Christopher brought his hands and the two upper corners of the handkerchief together. Two corners in each hand, he held the bandanna so that it hung doubled upon itself. He shook it gently, tilting one end downward over the hat, calling upon the Irish lad to watch sharply. Suddenly he said:

"There it comes, Tim! It's just peeping out of the fold—an egg! I'll drop it into the hat—there!"

An egg had appeared, in fact, in the fold of the handkerchief; it rolled gently into John Christopher's hat. While Tim Donovan stared in amazement, Jimmy Christopher showed his hands empty and again displayed both sides of the bandanna. Holding it again by its upper corners, he brought them together again, folded it, held it so that the fold was horizontal, and again shook it gently.

"Another one is coming, Tim! Yes! There it is! See it? I'll drop it into the hat beside the other. That makes two eggs in the hat! And the handkerchief, and my hands, as you see, conceal nothing!"

Smiling, Operator 5 repeated the procedure. Again folding the handkerchief, again shaking it, he caused an egg to appear. A third, a fourth, a fifth time he performed the mysterious ritual. Tim Donovan's eyes widened in puzzlement.

"Now—a sixth egg, Tim! There it is! I drop it into the hat, as before. I show the bandanna and my hands empty. Six will be enough, I think." He folded the handkerchief together and stuffed it into his pocket. "Six eggs in the hat, Tim. Are you a good catcher? Here they come!"

With a sudden movement, Jimmy Christopher tossed the hat at the startled boy. Tim Donovan grabbed at it frantically, expecting to hear the breaking of fragile egg-shells. The hat crushed together in his chubby hands and he stared into it in blank amazement. It was empty!

"They're gone, Jimmy! All six!"

"They must have vanished into thin air while the hat was coming at you, then!" Jimmy Christopher chuckled. "Figure that one out, Tim!"

"Golly!" the boy exclaimed.

OPERATOR 5 left Tim examining the hat while he strode to the telephone. He lifted the receiver; he hesitated and replaced it. Anxiety darkened his eyes as he returned to the chair beside his father.

"The danger to Di, the menace of the Master of Death's plan—that isn't all, Dad. Kalmar's early experiments in resurrection, when he had not yet perfected his technique, produced madmen. Those maniacs are killers. Kalmar uses them, I'm positive, as his agents of destruction. There must be scores of them hiding—scores that steal out into the night to do Kalmar's bidding. The menace of madmen loose in our cities is great enough—but the Master of Death has ruthlessly added to it!"

"My boy," John Christopher sighed, "I am almost ready to believe that a man who possesses such powers might be forgiven any crime he might commit."

"Not the crime of creating a populace of soulless living corpses, Dad!"

Ex-Operator Q-6 lapsed into a brooding silence. Tim Donovan tugged eagerly at Jimmy Christopher's arm. "How'd you do that trick, Jimmy?" he asked curiously. "I can't figure it out!"

Operator 5 smiled slowly and withdrew the folded bandanna

from his pocket. "Here's the whole secret, Tim—and it's very simple." He displayed the device which made the magical effect possible. It was an ordinary egg from which the contents had been blown, attached to one edge of the handkerchief with a black silk thread.

"There weren't six eggs at all, Tim—there was never more than one. I made you believe there were six, but it was simply the same egg appearing over and over again. Now, stand behind me while I do it again, and you'll see how it works."

OPERATOR 5 replaced the hat on the table while Tim watched at his side. He began by tucking the hollow egg out of sight inside his unbuttoned coat. The thread reaching from the concealed shell to the edge of the bandanna was invisible. Jimmy Christopher held the handkerchief up by two corners.

"The preparation of the egg is simple. Simply tap two small holes through the shell of any egg, one on each end. Blow out the white and the yolk. Insert through one hole a piece of match half an inch long, with one end of the thread tied to its middle. Plug up both holes in the shell with ordinary candle wax. The egg then has the thread fastened to it. The length of the thread is about two thirds the length of one side of the handkerchief. The other end of it is sewn to an edge midway between two corners.

"I hold the bandanna, as you see, with the edge to which the thread is attached uppermost. I show the handkerchief on both sides while the egg stays concealed under my coat. When I move my hands outward a few inches, the egg is pulled from my coat. It hangs out of sight behind the handkerchief. Folding the two upper corners of the handkerchief together and holding them in one hand, then taking the other two corners in the other hand, I jiggle the bandanna until the egg drops into the hat."

"I see, Jimmy!" the boy exclaimed.

"While the egg is in the hat, I show the handkerchief again back and front. Holding it by the same two corners as at first, I lift it. The egg leaves the hat and again hangs behind the bandanna. These actions are then repeated as many times as you please. At the finish, I fold the bandanna with the shell inside it, unseen, and tuck it away. There you are, Tim—you can do it easily."

"Gosh, Jimmy! That's swell!" the boy said gleefully as he took the prepared bandanna and studied it.

Suddenly Operator 5 strode off to the telephone. Again he called the secret number of headquarters B-3; again he obtained connection with Z-7.

"The body of Chancellor Ulreck," he questioned, "has not yet been claimed?"

"Not yet!"

"There's only one possible reason for that, Chief. One of the wearers of the golden crown, an agent in the Master of Death's espionage system, is on watch. He knows that F-4 is waiting. He will not claim the body while our operator is there. We must try a new tactic, Chief! Call F-4 off the watch in exactly thirty minutes. I'll handle that detail in my own way. It's our only chance that Ulreck's body will lead us to Kalmar."

Operator 5 turned briskly away from the telephone and peered at Tim Donovan. "I've got a job for you, fellow—the most important you ever faced. Diane's safety may depend on it,

Tim. Hop into a taxi immediately. Go to the Customs building. When F-4 leaves, you're to watch the box containing Chancellor Ulreck's body. Be extremely careful not to appear to be watching it. I'm gambling that Kalmar's agents do not know you, Tim."

"I'm off!" the boy exclaimed.

Operator 5's lips tightened grimly as the Irish lad eagerly pulled on his cap and ran down the stairs. He heard the entrance door click; the surge of a motor followed.

Jimmy Christopher strode back into his workshop. He returned holding a small, black tube in his hand—an object which appeared to be a fountain-pen with an unusually large clip. He thrust it into his vest pocket, tugged on his hat, strode to the outer door, and paused peering into John Christopher's face.

Ex-Operator Q-6 sat motionless, peering into space, while Operator 5's steps sounded on the stairs and the entrance opened and closed. A gleam came into his eyes—a glitter of desperate hope. His lips formed words that sounded husky whispers in the stillness of the room.

"No death!… No death!"

TO THE young man who alighted from a taxi in front of a staid apartment-house in the East Sixties, in New York, the doorman said: "Good evening, Mr. Walsh!"

"Good evening," Jimmy Christopher said.

An elevator carried him to the eleventh floor; a key, of which no duplicate existed, admitted him through a door that was steel, paneled with mahogany. He stepped into the bedroom of a quiet apartment and swung toward the window a strange contrivance consisting of a drum around which a rope ladder was coiled, a motor, a ratchet, a long gooseneck to which a black box was affixed; it was bolted to an anchored table. Operator 5 lowered forty feet of the ladder over the sill, into the darkness of the night, and climbed upon it.

He descended into the passageway; he swung to the balcony of an adjoining building. He shot the beam of his flashlight upward and it struck the lens of the black box protruding over the sill. The gleam actuated a photo-electric cell; while the motor hummed, the ladder coiled out of sight and the window slid shut. Turning, Operator 5 entered a quiet room and stepped through a door into a corridor.

Operator 5 approached another door which bore the name-plate: *Carleton Victor.* Victor, all the world knew, was a photo-portraitist of unrivaled reputation who maintained sumptuous studios on Fifth Avenue. The great of the world came to him for the privilege of sitting before his lens. A portrait signed with Victor's name was a credential of importance; he chose his subjects carefully. Now, in answer to Jimmy Christopher's ring, the door of the artist's penthouse opened.

"Good evening, Mr. Victor," said the manservant who stepped back respectfully.

Operator 5 passed his hat to Crowe, gentleman's gentleman extraordinary. "You are well, I hope, Crowe?" he asked solicitously.

"Oh, yes, sir!" Crowe said. "I am in excellent health, sir."

"That," said Carleton Victor, "is good to hear. I should miss you sadly, Crowe, if ever anything happened to you. Still, should you meet a sudden end, I think I should insist upon your services just the same, following your resurrection,"

Crowe paled. "My—what, sir?" he asked, appalled.

He received no answer, because Carleton Victor had opened the door of a closet and stepped into it, closing it tightly. The closet was thoroughly soundproofed; it contained only a telephone. It was an instrument used only by Operator 5, never by Carleton Victor. Jimmy Christopher quickly called headquarters B-3, exchanged signals, and switched into the line a frequency distorter which made eavesdropping impossible.

Z-7's voice rang immediately the connection was completed. "I have had word from Tim Donovan! Soon after F-4 left the Customs building, a truck drew up and two men claimed the box containing Chancellor Ulreck's body! They were allowed to take it. Tim managed to telephone me just before he started following it!"

"Thank God for that!" Jimmy Christopher exclaimed. "Tim will stick on that trail, Chief! He's a better shadower than any operator in the service. When he reports, I want the call switched through to me here!"

"Very well!" Z-7 agreed. "We are expecting word any moment! In the meantime, I have new reports here which may pertain to the plans of the Master of Death. For instance, I have information that Governor Glendon has become afflicted with general amnesia. He has heart trouble; he suffered a serious stroke and a newspaper was about to publish a report of his death when word reached them that the collapse was not fatal. At the same time, I have an almost exactly similar report concerning Major-General Rosson, Chief of Staff of the U.S. Army and Navy!

"General Rosson, driving his car along a highway during a violent storm a week ago, was struck by a falling high-tension wire. He was thought to be dead and taken to his home. Surprisingly, he reappeared at his office two days later, apparently unharmed. Still, he appears to have changed. His memory is faulty. His entire attitude toward the service is a constant challenge. It is threatening to disrupt the functioning of the General Staff! This may mean nothing, Operator 5, but—"

"It means a great deal, Chief," Operator 5 said quietly. "It means—" He hesitated. "Good Lord, Chief! If Dr. Kalmar controls the minds of our key men, he will be the Master of the Nation!"

Z-7 blurted: "God! Is it possible that already—"

"Nothing is impossible to Dr. Kalmar! Order Governor Glendon and General Rosson watched constantly, Chief! Try to learn if other key men are in a similar situation. Work fast!"

JIMMY CHRISTOPHER turned grimly from the telephone. He was about to step out when a shrill clatter of the bell stopped him. Swiftly he brought the receiver to his ear. Tim Donovan's voice rang over the wire:

"Jimmy! Jimmy, I've spotted the place where Chancellor Ulreck's body has been taken! It was just carried in!"

"The address, Tim!" Operator 5 demanded tightly.

The boy gave it rapidly. "It's a big house on upper Riverside Drive! There are people coming to it—men and women—by the score! They leave their cars down the drive and come on foot—

more and more every minute! And Jimmy—I saw a symbol over the door of that house! It's a golden crown!"

Operator 5's voice took on an edge. "Stay on the Drive, Tim! Keep watching that house. I'm coming!"

He disconnected quickly. Immediately he called secret headquarters B-3 again. He repeated the conversation to Z-7, and continued: "There's no doubt that the house on Riverside Drive is one of Dr. Kalmar's headquarters! He may have Diane Elliot there with him now. Issue orders to every agent available in New York, Chief!

"Send them in cars to that address. They are to wait for me. God only knows what is going on inside that house tonight. On the job, Chief—and wait for me!"

Operator 5's face was pale and drawn as he gripped the inner knob of the soundproofed closet; Carleton Victor's lips were hard-pressed when he stepped out. At his gesture, Crowe brought his hat. He turned to the outer door and paused as the manservant observed in his dry voice:

"Beg pardon, sir. A rather strange caller came today. He professed wanting to see you, sir, yet he seemed more interested in talking to me. It seems, sir, if I understand rightly, that this man's family has been visited by a miracle. His sister, sir—a young girl—was accidentally asphyxiated by illuminating gas only a few nights ago. He swears she was dead when they found her, sir. Yet he made the astounding statement that she is living and well today—that she was brought back to life by a man who possesses mystic powers to revive the dead."

Carleton Victor asked quietly: "Do you believe it, Crowe?"

116

Crowe blinked. "Of course, sir, I hardly—but the man was sincere, sir. I could not doubt him. He spoke so reverently of this miracle worker—one called the Master of Death. He declared that one need never fear death if one follows the Master. He urged me to see for myself."

"You wish to do so, Crowe?" Jimmy Christopher demanded.

"I confess, sir, I am so fascinated that—that I should like the evening, sir, if I may."

"Crowe," Carleton Victor said with a snap, "you may not have the evening! You will stay here, in these rooms, and wait for my return. Furthermore, you will forget what you have heard. Every word of it, Crowe! Do you understand?"

Crowe's face flashed pale. "Yes, sir! But, sir—"

"Forget it, Crowe, unless you wish to become the witless slave of one of the most evil men who ever walked the face of the earth!"

Carleton Victor stepped out suddenly. The click of the bolt shocked a jerk from the usually imperturbable Crowe. The man-servant stood pale as death, staring at the closed door and he repeated in breathless horror:

" 'Become a witless slave—!' "

CHAPTER 9
HOUSE OF RESURRECTION

THE HUM of the city was hushed; the glare of the streets was dimmed, where Riverside Drive curved close to the Hudson in a comparatively unsettled district. The lights of the great George Washington Bridge twinkled below the bend at which scores of cars were parked. No occupant remained in any of them. From them, men and women had hurried, to a stone stairway which ascended through a high wall to terraced grounds above. In thick gloom, a huge house sat, faint light shining through the drapes of its windows—dark save for a symbol outlined upon a blood-red pane above the entrance.

A royal crown!

Operator 5, leaving his roadster in the line of automobiles, hurried along the edge of the park while he watched the house. Out of the darkness figures hastened toward him. Tim Donovan, breaking into a run, gripped his hand and swung into step.

"They've kept coming constantly while we waited for you, Jimmy!" he exclaimed. "There must be several hundred people in that house now!"

Jimmy Christopher turned as Z-7 approached. Behind the Washington chief came a group of men. Their faces were shaded by low-pulled hats; their manner was cautious, wary; they were picked operators in the Intelligence Service. Behind them, a second group waited. Operator 5 counted their number and his hand strayed unconsciously to the golden death-charm on his watch-chain.

"A daring move of Kalmar's, Chief—operating so nearly in the open. He is becoming supremely confident of his power. These people have been drawn to him by skilled propaganda spreaders. They have been circulating through the city, urging those who were impressed by their stories to attend this secret meeting tonight. By word of mouth, the Master of Death is spreading his devilish gospel—and here are the results!"

Z-7 asked quietly: "What are your plans, Operator 5?"

"Those people, Chief," Operator 5 continued, "are assuredly sworn to secrecy. They must have been told a password—but, you may depend on it, fear seals their lips. We must plan a surprise move. I want our men to station themselves around the grounds and wait for my signal.

"I'll try to enter. If I succeed, I will give the signal at the proper moment, with this flare." He removed from his pocket the black tube which appeared to be a fountain-pen. "I designed it for a purpose such as this. One end is weighted with lead. A pull on the trigger ignites a magnesium charge. I intend, if possible, to hurl it out through a window after tripping it. When you see a red light—close in on that house!"

Z-7 CALLED his men about him as Operator 5 began to cross the drive. He slowed his steps when he saw two men and two women hurrying toward the base of the stairway; in surprise he noted that they had left an expensive, imported car—that they were wearing evening dress. He allowed them to mount the long flight of stairs ahead of him. He peered into the gloom alertly as he neared the landing.

Out of the shadows, a man stepped warily. He spoke in a low tone, and the four answered in whispered words which Operator 5 could not distinguish. They hurried on, toward the door above which the golden crown gleamed. Operator 5's muscles tightened as he mounted the last step. From the darkness, the sentry stepped again.

He was a hulking figure in the night. The crimson gleam from the doorway colored his hollow-cheeked face gauntly. His was a vacant stare. And on the lapel of his coat, Jimmy Christopher noted, he was wearing the emblem of the golden crown.

He demanded: "The word?"

Operator 5 answered softly: "Immortality."

"That is not—!"

The words choked off in the big man's throat as Jimmy Christopher struck. His stiff fingers shot to the sentry's neck. Odorous breath exploded in his face as the huge man stiffened and began to topple. Operator 5's swift glance swept the grounds; he caught the sentry's arms. Quickly, every sense alert, he dragged the man to the deep shadow hovering beneath an old tree.

He listened and heard no sound. No alarm came out of the night. Operator 5's attack had been swift and silent. He stooped and detached the symbol of the golden crown from the unconscious man's coat. He affixed it on his own lapel. He hurried back to the head of the stone flight, his fingers seeking a reassuring touch of his armpit-holstered automatic. He strode, then, straight toward the door above which the golden crown gleamed against its background of blood-red.

As he neared the door, two men stepped from the shadows, peering into his face. They were also wearing the symbol of the crown. Their eyes glinted at the ornament on Operator 5's lapel. One of them demanded throatily:

"Your number?"

"Ninety-four."

They blinked, they withdrew. Operator 5's pulse speeded as

he reached for the knob of the door over which crimson light streamed. It turned before he touched it. The entrance opened wide; he stepped through.

He found himself inside red-draped walls, facing another gaunt-faced man who wore the symbol of the golden crown. From beyond the crimson curtain came a bustle of movement through air tightened with a sense of awesome expectancy.

The sentinel at the door peered at Operator 5, but made no move toward him. Jimmy Christopher felt the chill of danger as he parted the scarlet drapes. He entered a dimly lighted corridor; he turned to peer through a broad arch. Beyond it lay a spacious, vaulted room, rustling with quiet sounds, filled by men and women seated in gilded pews—a barbaric Temple of the Crown in the midst of the metropolis!

IN THE doorway Operator 5 paused. The dim light which suffused the air reflected crimson from the curtained walls. At the far end, a platform was raised, and behind it, another red curtain hung, also decorated with the symbol of the crown. It was empty, yet the eyes of every man and woman in the gathering were turned toward it in reverent anticipation of the appearance of a presence hinted by the fluttering of the blood-red folds....

Suddenly, the muted reverberations of a gong vibrated through the temple. Its note hushed every faint movement into silence. The tone swelled solemnly and died away; a second time it came; a third. And as the third stroke of the gong faded, the sound of muffled footfalls beat behind Operator 5.

He stepped aside, watching four men who were approach-

The Master of Death thundered forbiddingly: "I need utter only one command and these men will tear you limb from limb!"

ing—four men bearing a litter between them. They were wearing crimson armbands marked with the crown; they were carrying a still form which lay beneath a crimson shroud. The silk rustled and the golden fringe twinkled as they passed through the arch into the temple. Operator 5 saw, lying beneath the cloth marked with the mystic insignia, a girl whose face was waxy in death....

Down the aisle, between the pews, the four men carried their burden of death. As the even rhythm of their footfalls reverberated, a singing note came from the lips of many who watched the approach of the corpse. It rose in volume; it was taken up by others until every member of the congregation echoed it. It became a wordless chant, a lament that rang with hope. Louder and louder it grew, while the litter-bearers mounted the platform and placed the dead body on its center.

Behind the still girl, the crimson curtains stirred anew. The chant became hushed. Through the folds stepped a man garbed in a garment of crimson. He was not masked; he was not the Master of Death. In the dim, red light, Operator 5 recognized the features of the man who had called himself Karant. The red-clothed figure advanced to a position beside the dead girl and raised his hands for silence.

When silence settled in the vaulted chamber, Karant's hollow voice carried into the vastness of the crimson-walled temple:

"Disciples of the Master of Death!"

He brought from the folds of his robe a rolled parchment. He spread it before him and read in sepulchral tones.

"Before you lies one whom the Darkness has taken—one who abandoned herself to eternity. To the world she is dead; to the worshipers of the Master of Death she merely sleeps. The power of the Master will cause her to rise; the power of the Master will return her to life!"

Again, heavy silence reigned. "Unto himself the Master of Death will take this child and bid her live again. His will to make her live is greater than hers was to make her to destroy her own life. His benediction is stronger than the waters into which she plunged herself. Six hours the Darkness has held her—yet it will yield and vanish at the invocation of the Master!

"We await the Master of Death!"

The hollow-voiced man vanished through the folds of the silken curtain. Alone on the platform, before the eyes of the worshipers in the temple, lay the body of a girl who had chosen to end her life by drowning. Again, from every lip, the deep tones of the wordless chant rose to tremble the walls—a cry of awesome hope....

OPERATOR 5 moved quietly toward a pew at the rear. A step startled him. A touch on his shoulder brought him to a pause. He turned to peer into the deep-set eyes of a man wearing an armband marked with the crown. A throaty voice asked him: "You are Ninety-four?"

Tensely, Operator 5 answered: "Yes!"

"The Master has requested the presence of Ninety-four. You will come."

The wearer of the arm-band turned away. A new dread struck Operator 5's heart as he hesitated. He had identified himself as Ninety-four at random; to refuse to follow the man who had summoned him would create suspicion. He suspected a trick;

yet he was obliged to chance obedience. He strode through the arch as the chanting continued, following the man with the arm-band down the dark corridor.

At a door, Jimmy Christopher's escort paused, hand on the knob. "The Master awaits you," he said quietly, and opened the way. Operator 5 tensed as he crossed the sill. He entered a handsomely furnished study—empty. He glanced around warily—and jerked. A click told him that the door had become bolted behind him. He turned slowly, feeling that the gaze of unseen eyes was upon him.

Suddenly the lights went out! Jimmy Christopher whipped about as quick movements rustled. Heels thudded. Rushing noises closed in upon him. He darted aside quickly, and a groping arm struck across his face. Instantly a stifled shout sounded; heavy bodies crushed around Operator 5. He struck out powerfully and his knuckles clicked; he tore back, striving to free himself of the hands that gripped his arms. He struggled frantically against a mounting power too great for any man to combat....

In hands that clamped him like vises he was held motionless. Footfalls sounded again. A sharp click brought light into the room. The glare stung Operator 5's eyes as he gazed grimly at the men who held him prisoner. Their faces were alight with a mad ferocity. Each of them wore the emblem of the golden crown. They were men who were mad!

Rigidly they held Jimmy Christopher as a silken sound came from an open door. A garment fluttered across the sill. Into the room strode a man garbed in a robe of red, a man whose head was masked by a red hood. Operator 5 peered at him coldly as he took slow, gliding steps and paused. He met unflinchingly the Master of Death's icy gaze.

"Ninety-four," Dr. Anton Kalmar's husky voice came, "is one of my lieutenants now busy in another room. You have made a sad error, Operator 5!"

Jimmy Christopher answered tightly: "That I admit. But you are making a far graver error, Dr—"

"Hold your silence!" The Master of Death thundered forbiddingly. "I need utter only one command and these men will tear you limb from limb. They revel in savage destruction. They are my Corps of Destroyers."

The Master of Death stepped back. "Take him away!" he commanded. "Follow me with him!"

THE RED robe rustled as the Master of Death turned from the room. The men gripping Operator 5's arms forced him between them through the door. They passed into the corridor. The crimson figure entered a huge room that was gleaming white—a tiled laboratory filled with strange devices—and paused.

"Bind him!" The savage strength of the madmen drew Operator 5 back to the wall. He felt ropes whipped around his wrists and ankles; he felt the cold metal of iron rings, studded into the wall. His captors did their work swiftly; they retreated leaving him bound. At a sharp command, they herded from the room like unthinking animals; and Operator 5 faced the Master of Death alone.

The red-robed figure declared grimly: "I offered you a bargain. Now your time has expired!"

He stepped forward. His red-gloved hands drew Jimmy Christopher's automatic. He sought further for other weapons. His fingertips closed upon the tip of the tube which seemed to be a fountain-pen; they loosened and moved on. Jimmy Christopher's lips tightened imperceptibly as the Master of Death drew back.

"You have learned much, Operator 5," the grave voice came. "But you are helpless to hinder me.... Do you hear that voice—the voice of hundreds raised in praise of me? They worship me as a god. Their numbers will swell to millions. All this nation will worship me—and make me King!"

Operator 5 peered in cold fascination at the hooded man.

Dr. Kalmar continued: "I choose to inform you how hopeless are your attacks upon me. Listen! Do you know that I have serving me many squads of Empire Builders—men and women who have died, whom I have caused to live again, who are devoting themselves to the solidifying of my coming Kingdom? I have sent out into the world countless ambassadors—men who have died unknown to their fellows, who live again through my power!"

The red figure moved toward the opposite wall, in which was framed a closed window. The red hand reached for the latch that fastened it.

"Tonight the ranks of my worshipers is growing. They will see a dead girl rise to live again and they will bow before my power. They will see me take a soul into my hands from a living body and place it within a resurrected corpse. The soul of a girl for the body of a girl! The soul of—!"

The red hand raised the panel. Through shining glass, Operator 5 peered into an adjoining room. It was brightly lighted; and as the blind raised, a movement appeared. A girl hurried to the window and peered through. Into her face the light gleamed whitely. And from the lips of Operator 5 a name burst: "Diane!"

DIANE ELLIOT pressed her hands pleadingly against the glass; her lips moved as she called to Jimmy Christopher, but no sound penetrated the panes. Her eyes widened in terror at the man garbed in crimson; she recoiled before the glint of his eyes. She peered again at Operator 5, beseeching help—and suddenly she was shut from sight as the leaf of the window was lowered again.

"Her soul!" the Master of Death chortled.

Jimmy Christopher strained at the ropes as the cloaked figure crossed the room to a door. The red hand opened it. Through the crimson hood, Dr. Kalmar commanded:

"Come! Come quickly!"

Through the doorway, a man stepped; Operator 5 stiffened with consternation. In the doorway the small figure stood, turning to Jimmy Christopher a face pale and waxy. The dulled eyes gazed as if in a dream. At a gesture from the Master of Death, the man stepped forward obediently into the brighter light. Operator 5 peered fascinated at a man whom he had seen lying dead in a casket—a man who had been a corpse ten days, yet who now lived again.

Chancellor Ulreck!

"Gaze upon him!" the figure in crimson ordered. "Gaze upon a creation of my power! Witness a man who will carry my message across the sea, who will aid in spreading it over all the world! I have granted him new life, and he will devote that life to my worship." He whirled upon the quiet man. "Is it not true?"

From the numb lips, the meek answer came: "Yes, Master."

"Go, now! Go back!"

The living dead man who had been the Chancellor of Dalgary obediently returned through the door and closed it. The Master of Death peered intently at Operator 5 and moved closer.

"You doubtless know that my process is the outstanding achievement of medical science. You know in part the means I have used. These teeter-boards. This artificial heart. In these bottles—the power of new life: heparin, an extract of liver, used to prevent the clotting of blood; epinephedrine and amyl-nitrite to constrict the small blood-vessels in order to build up the necessary pressure. Gum arabic, to prevent the diffusion of blood into the tissues until life has returned to the dead. Saline solutions." Dr. Kalmar paused. "But none of these restores the brain—none of them wipes away the numbing effect of death. This—this is my triumph!"

The red hand gripped a heavy-walled bottle and lifted it from a shelf. It bore no label, but within it rippled the golden fluid which Operator 5 had seen cause an excised heart to beat, which had aided a severed head to live. Its color glittered brightly in the light as the Master of Death returned it to its place.

"I alone know its secret! No one else will ever learn it! It is a blessed potion you shall never taste. You will never know a second life! You will know only destruction—a death without end!"

The Master of Death turned to a drawer; from it he lifted a gas-mask. He brought it closer to Operator 5.

"You have seen a man destroyed who was dangerous to me— his heart cut out. You have seen another removed—his head cut off. You have seen still another comrade shot through the brain. A bullet in the brain does not entirely remove the promise of resurrection. The heart stripped from the body makes eternal death certain. Level by level, I choose my means of destroying my foes. So I destroy them. So I number the images of Yama that mark their eternal deaths…!"

AT OPERATOR 5'S feet the Master of Death dropped the weird gas-mask. "For my most dangerous enemies I reserve the Seventh and Highest Level of Eternal Death. It destroys more horribly than the Sixth, which is dissolution in powerful acid. It eats away your body while you live. It exposes you to attack by the deadliest of bacteria. It brings to you a rotting death—lets you see yourself disintegrate. With the Seventh Level of Eternal Death, Operator 5, I honor you!"

The red hand of the Master rose to a lever affixed to the wall. "You need not fear immediate pain. You will scarcely know that you have been touched—at first. I need only tell you that you will be bathed in an invisible gas called Yperite, mustard gas, or technically dichlorethyl sulphide!"

Jimmy Christopher straightened tightly in his bonds.

"It can kill instantly—but I do not mean to kill you quickly. It will soon issue into this room, through the vents near the ceiling, to fill this air-tight space. I have placed this gas-mask at your disposal. Its aspirator will allow you to breathe safely. But—the gas will penetrate your clothing, cling to your skin. Your body, during the following days, will become covered with blisters that will open into raw sores—you will see yourself decay—slowly you will rot and die!"

The Master of Death moved the brass lever, and instantly the room was filled with a hissing sound!

The red-robed figure moved swiftly to Operator 5. The crimson-gloved hand brought a gleaming knife blade from the folds of the cloak. The edge bit into the ropes that bound Jimmy Christopher's left hand. The strands dropped free as the Master whirled away. He spun the knife; its point drove into the floor at Operator 5's feet. He sped to the door, jerked it open, and passed through. Instantly it shut snugly, and a bolt clicked hard into its socket. From vents in the ceiling, the invisible poison poured....

CHAPTER 10
THE POWER OF THE CROWN

OPERATOR 5 twisted desperately from the wall, reaching his free hand toward the knife that quivered in the wood at his feet. He seized its hilt; he slashed the blade against the strands binding his ankles. He stepped away and the steel flashed again to free his right hand. He dropped the knife and snatched up the gas-mask that lay beyond.

He affixed it swiftly, pinching the clamp on his nose, breathing through the aspirator. He whirled to the door and found it firmly fastened. He sped to the other and threw his weight against it; it did not jar in its frame. A chill gathered around his heart as he backed away. Through the rubberized fabric of the mask he heard the hissing grow louder—the sibilant song of the deadly gas pouring into the room…!

Frantically, Jimmy Christopher peered around at the carboys on the floor, at the bottles on the shelves. He knew that the Master of Death had not exaggerated the effects of the deadly dichlorethyl sulphide. Once it touched his skin, Jimmy Christopher realized, nothing could stay its ghastly effect. He stepped along the shelves, rapidly reading the Latin labels on the bottles, peering through the grotesque lenses of the mask….

The pipes carrying the invisible poison into the room, he knew, must lead to compressor-tanks somewhere beyond. Before the gas could reach an effective strength, the air in the tubes must be exhausted, the poison must circulate. Each motion he made would aid in the saturation of the air, but he continued his rapid search.

His hand darted to the neck of a heavy bottle sitting on the laboratory table. Its label read simply: *Mineral Oil.* He twisted the cork loose. He lifted the bottle above his head and sent the viscid stuff pouring down upon him. Deliberately he streamed it upon his clothing. He tore open his collar and directed the thick stream against his skin. He immersed his hands in it; he rubbed them over the skin unprotected by the mask. While the hissing noise continued—while the power of the gas crept into the air—he emptied the bottle upon himself, until the oil soaked him to the skin….

He backed away, breathing laboriously through the aspirator, making doubly sure that his body was completely covered by the thick fluid. He remained pressed against the wall, striving to listen through the fabric of the mask. The hissing continued—a venomous sound. For a long time, Operator 5 remained motionless, daring to hope that the film of oil covering his body would shield him from the poison while the gas poured in. For an eternity he did not move—until, at last, the hissing sound changed to a lower note.

Operator 5 felt a new current flowing through the air of the room, and realized that a ventilator was working, drawing the poisoned air outward. The vents were no longer spewing the horrible agent of destruction; the new sound was coming from larger openings flush with the laboratory floor. The air churned and a low bubbling sound was audible below—the exhaust passing through an absorptive liquid. While the air grew clearer, Jimmy Christopher listened at the door; and he heard the muffled sounds of footfalls. Beyond, rising to a hysterical pitch, swelled the chanting voice of the hundreds in the Temple of the Crown.

Somewhere nearby, a door-latch clicked. A voice commanded in muffled tone: "Bring her out! We are ready for the ceremony!" Swiftly Jimmy Christopher crossed to the side wall. With one oil-drenched hand he unlatched the shuttered window. He raised the leaf slowly, bending his head low to the narrow crack. He peered into stronger light, into the room where Diane Elliot was held prisoner.

INTO THAT room, two men had come—men of powerful

frame, wearing crimson bands on their arms. The girl recoiled in terror as they advanced. They crowded her into a corner while she cried protests which Operator 5 could not hear. They seized her; and as they drew her away, she lifted her chin defiantly. Her eyes were a challenge; she ceased her protest. She went toward the door without resistance—toward the fate of *Yajna!*

Operator 5 whirled away grimly. Again, outside his door, there was the sound of footfalls. Dr. Kalmar's deep voice ordered gruffly:

"Allow him to come out! Allow him to escape if he wishes. The room is now clear, but do not touch him. Your hands will rot away if you touch him! At once—release him!"

Operator 5 tore the mask from his head and breathed cold, clean air. His oiled hand moved unconsciously to his empty armpit holster; he swiftly glanced around the laboratory in search of his automatic, but it was gone. The Master of Death had taken it. The footfalls moved near the laboratory door.

Operator 5 slipped from his vest-pocket the short black tube. He held it poised as the bolt of the door drew back. He sprang the trip; he hurled it straight across the room. Its weighted end crashed against the pane of the window. Glass shattered as it whirled through. Instantly a bright red gleam appeared outside—a glare that grew blindingly bright.

The laboratory door swung open. Into the room strode two men wearing crimson arm-bands. They stopped short, peering at the window through which the scarlet gleam shone. They spun to face Operator 5. They grabbed toward their hip-pockets; and at the same instant, Operator 5 acted.

He snatched at the buckle of his belt and clicked it loose. He snapped it from its loops. It sprang straight. The narrow sheath flew into the air, baring a supple rapier. Jimmy Christopher whipped the Toledo blade downward as the two lieutenants of the Master of Death jerked guns toward him.

His hissing blade lashed a furious power at the hands gripping the automatics. It darted from one to the other, and at the touch of its keen blade, blood flowed. Cries of dismay broke from the lips of the two as their fingers went numb and powerless under the whip of the steel. Metal sparkled against metal as Operator 5's swift maneuver whipped the rapier to the guns and jerked them away as if with a force of black magic.

The sweep of his blade spilled the two men backward as he spun to the door. He leaped through, pulling the knob; he shot the bolt into its socket. He whirled to peer along the corridor. At its far end, near the entrance of the temple, other men wearing arm-bands were stationed. Two of them were gripping Diane Elliot's arms. Near the girl, the crimson-robed figure of the Master of Death was towering.

"Stations!" the muffled voice commanded.

Outside the house, sharp shouts sounded. Across the grass, quick steps slashed. Upon the porch, heavy heels thudded. The voice of Z-7 called: "Break it in!" The corps of Intelligence agents were responding to Operator 5's signal-flare; they were closing around the house. Guns crashed into the silence. The entrance jarred and creaked as heavy shoulders struck it from the outside. And as the sounds of the attack penetrated into the house of the living-dead, the Master of Death shouted another sharp command.

"Quick!"

OPERATOR 5 hurried along the corridor as the men wearing the crimson arm-bands scattered. One jerked open the drawer of a cabinet in the hall. Another lowered the leaf of a receptacle in the wall near the temple entrance. They backed away with hands gripping black glass spheres. As the Master of Death shouted again, they hurled the balls against the walls, rained them into the temple, toward the entrance, into the adjacent rooms.

Instantly, thick white fumes swelled into the air. Cold apprehension filled Operator 5 as he darted toward the red-robed man. A wisp of the gas reached his nostrils, carrying a strange odor. It was not any poison vapor that Operator 5 knew. It gusted up in a blinding vapor, harmless to life but baffling to the eyes. A smoke screen! In a second, the fog swelled to fill all the air, blurring the red-robed figure and the girl near him under a thickening cloud.

The Master of Death spun about as a fresh attack struck the entrance, as the panes of the windows in the Temple crashed inward. Operator 5 sprang through the mist. Diane Elliot glimpsed him and called his name in frantic hope. The two men who gripped her arms leaped toward Jimmy Christopher, jerking out automatics. In the dimming light, his rapier lashed.

Sharp cries sounded as the blade flicked, as blood spurted from the hands that swung the guns. Again the keen edge struck, whipping burning pain into the arms of the men who held

Diane. They retreated in terror as the girl tore away. They became almost invisible in the choking fumes as Operator 5 darted on, his rapier raised, striking toward the spot where the Master of Death had stood.

A sharp crash sounded as the entrance burst open. Unseen in the cloud, Intelligence men crowded forward. "Jimmy!" Tim Donovan called anxiously. "Jimmy!" he cried again—and the vapor engulfed him. Operator 5 lashed his rapier and quickly retreated from the arch. As a thicker cloud of mist rolled around him, he felt Diane Elliot grip his hand, and heard the sounds of tramping feet as the crowd in the Temple stampeded in terror.

Through the arch, the devotees of the Master of Death rushed in frantic fear. They were an invisible herd in the cloud, massing blindly toward the open entrance. Screams sounded from the throats of women; hoarse cries of rage tore from the lips of desperate men. Cold and grim, Operator 5 kept his position to avoid being swept into the crowd, to avoid striking any of his own men with his keen rapier in the eye-baffling smoke.

"Stick close, Diane!" Gripping her hand, he struggled across the hallway and found his way into a room opposite. Here the mist was as thick as in the corridor. He groped to the wall; he felt a window-sill; he caught the back of a chair and swung it forcibly. Glass spattered outward. He kicked jagged edges from the frame, working blindly, and drew Diane to the opening. He helped her through and dropped out—into air thick with the same baffling fumes that filled the house.

Over all the grounds, the cloud was swirling, flowing down into the Drive. Through it, scores of people were frantically fighting their way. Some of them stumbled from the edge of the stone wall and fell to the sidewalk below. The stairway was crowded, seething with those in desperate flight. From below, the snarling of car-starters sounded. Headlamps shot their shafts into misted air that swallowed their light. Sky, river, drive—all were obscured by the choking smoke.

Operator 5, keeping Diane close at his side, sprang toward the entrance. The golden crown above the door was now a crimson blot in the fumes. He took position, his rapier gripped and ready, at the side of the porch. Grimly he strove to penetrate the mist as it swirled. Out of it came the hoarse voices of the Intelligence men who had charged into the Temple.

"Keep your positions!" Jimmy Christopher shouted through the bedlam. "Wait for the gas to clear!"

IN THE drive, scores of cars were crawling. Metal ripped, bumpers clashed, as they collided blindly. Other terrorized worshipers of the Master of Death were still mobbing out of the house. Confusion stirred the fog. Jimmy Christopher stood guard at the door, alert to catch the faintest flicker of crimson in the smoke….

Tense minutes brought a hush into the pandemonium. The wind sweeping from the river began to thin the mist. The lights inside the house became spots that steadily brightened. The yawning entrance became a black frame. Vague figures began to move through it—Intelligence operators searching for their quarry. Jimmy Christopher, keeping Diane Elliot with him, stepped inside swiftly.

Out of the thinning fog, Z-7 appeared. "Operator 5! Thank God you're safe!"

"Thank God Diane's safe!" Jimmy Christopher echoed. "Where is Tim, Chief?"

"He came in with us—hunting for you. It was impossible to follow anyone through this damned smoke! Kalmar—was he here?"

"Yes!" Operator 5 affirmed grimly. He raised his voice to carry orders to the hurrying secret agents. "First squad get outside the house! Watch all entrances! Second squad search all the rooms! Go over this place from attic to cellar! Make it fast!"

The movements of the men quickened. Half of them crowded out; the others scurried into the rooms along the hall. Jimmy Christopher peered into the lessening for and called.

"Tim! Tim, old-timer! Where are you?"

No answer came through the mist. His lips pinched, Operator 5 left Diane Elliot at Z-7's side, and hurried to join the search. He climbed stairs to find many rooms on the second and third floors of the house; but Tim was in none of them. He searched the laboratories on the ground floor; he hurried into a cellar that was crowded with weird, discarded apparatus for the resurrection of the, dead, but there was no sign of Tim. He returned grimly to the entrance.

"Tim!" he called again. "Tim!"

Again—no answer. Diane Elliot's gaze clung anxiously to Operator 5 as he strode into the study of the Master of Death. With Z-7 she followed. Into the room Intelligence agents hurried, blurting their reports.

"We've found twelve men, in cells! Crazy, all of them! They're under lock and by God we'll keep them there!"

"We've made a prisoner of the man you say is Chancellor Ulreck!"

"There is no sign of Dr. Kalmar!"

"Dr. Kalmar and his assistants got to their cars under cover of the smoke—they've gone!"

Operator 5 declared: "That was the purpose of his bombs! Send out a general radio alarm! Call Police Headquarters! Those men are to be arrested on sight! Keep searching this house—find Tim Donovan!"

As the men hurried off, Jimmy Christopher peered at the desk of the Master of Death. He jerked open drawers, brought out record books, scanned their pages. He turned away, his oil-smeared face haggard, his eyes shining darkly.

"Kalmar took Tim with him, Chief! It's the only answer. They've taken Tim!" His fist struck the desk. "There are records of Dr. Kalmar's experiments. There are documents to build a case against him—even entries of his sacrifices!… God, Chief! That human demon—"

He broke off as an Intelligence agent hurried into the room. "There's no, sign of the boy. He's not in this house or on these grounds!"

Operator 5 squared his shoulders "Take charge of your prisoners," he ordered. "Keep a guard around this house. Every particle of evidence here must be taken. We—"

He broke off and turned away. His lips tightened as he peered at a door at the far side of the room. He gestured caution as Z-7 was about to speak. Eyes fixed on the knob, he took slow steps toward the inner door. He had seen it move—move so slightly that it might have been a trick of vision. He had seen the knob twist—yet he could not be sure. He drew his rapier level. He seized the knob. Suddenly he twisted it and stepped back.

In the light, a white face shone—the face of a man backed into the closet. His head was bound with bandages. He stared out in terror. Operator 5 peered and his rapier lowered. Z-7, at Jimmy Christopher's shoulder, muttered with stricken amazement. They gazed spellbound at the man in the gloom.

He was one whom Operator 5 had seen shot through the head—one whom he had seen killed instantly. Yet that man stood living now before him. Operator X-11!

CHAPTER 11
THE MASTER STRIKES

THE DOOR of a bedroom in John Christopher's home swung open; Operator 5 strode out. His face was drawn, his eyes anxious. He had come to Address Y directly from the Temple of the Crown on Riverside Drive; he had cleaned the oil from his body with calm confidence that it had protected him from the deadly gas liberated by the Master of Death; he was garbed in fresh clothing. As he strode to the entrance, Diane Elliot seized his hand.

"Jimmy—oh, I'm so grateful! And yet I—I'm sorry. You brought me back only to lose him. I would rather—"

Operator 5 said huskily. "We're doing everything possible

to trace Tim, but—the Master of Death covers his tracks well. He's gone to some third rendezvous now. The devil only knows where it is, but I'll find it!"

"I know you will!" Diane agreed.

Jimmy Christopher's hand tightened on the girl's as he gazed at his father. Ex-Operator Q-6 was gazing at him rapidly, in a glowing absorption. The one-time secret agent came to his feet.

"Call on me for anything, Jimmy, but—?" His voice wavered. "Perhaps—perhaps the power that Dr. Kalmar holds is worth the existence of this government. Perhaps it is more precious than anything else on earth! To destroy that man—"

"That man," Jimmy Christopher declared firmly, "must be destroyed or he will destroy us all! His power over his followers must be broken! As for his secret, Dad, that cannot perish. The lengths to which he has gone will be reached by others—true men of science whose work is done for the welfare of the world. In the hands of such men it will become a blessing instead of a curse."

"Yet—"

"Dr. Ernest Martin Chesterly is another scientist who has gone far in the same field, Dad. He has just returned to this country. In Moscow he conducted experiments which promise to equal Dr. Kalmar's. He has come into possession of priceless information and he will use it for the benefit of mankind. It may be years before he can achieve exactly the same results as Dr. Kalmar—but it will come!"

Jimmy Christopher left his father absorbed in thought and

signaled Diane after him to the entrance. There he said quietly: "Watch Dad, Di! Watch him! Every moment!"

"I will, Jimmy! I understand! Jimmy—"

The girl's warm lips pressed impulsively to Operator 5's. She gazed deep into his eyes as she drew back wordlessly. He turned; he stepped out the entrance. The lines in his face were etched deep when he took the wheel of his roadster and sent it purring southward.

He entered the Vertex Building; he passed through the guarded doors of secret Intelligence headquarters B-3. He entered the chief's office and Z-7 gripped his hand.

"Thanks to you, we might have scored a complete victory tonight—except for Dr. Kalmar's devilish smoke-screen. We have taken some of his men prisoners. We have brought Chancellor Ulreck here—and X-11."

"The Chancellor," Operator 5 said softly, "may be returned to his family. They will understand that they must guard him now from the Master of Death. As for—"

The communications-room opened and the chief-dispatcher called:

"Telephone message for Operator 5—the chief's phone."

JIMMY CHRISTOPHER lifted the instrument to hear a cautious voice. "Operator 5, this is T-6 reporting. I have been following orders given me by Z-7, trying to pick up the trail of the ghouls working for the Master of Death. I received word a short time ago of the death of the son of J. Pomeroy Morrell."

Operator 5 tightened at the name. It was that of one of the richest men in the country—a banker of international renown whose financial influence was felt around the world. Morrell's name was synonymous with the most vital operations of national credit and finance. Jimmy Christopher urged: "Go on!"

"Today Morrell's young son was at the estate in Westchester. The boy slipped out of sight and remained missing for some hours. He was found under tragic circumstances. He had stolen away to go swimming in a small lake behind the estate. He had become caught in underbrush beneath the surface, and he drowned. This occurred only a short time ago. I learned of it when the local hospital was called. Attempts to revive him failed. The house is in a state of insane anxiety. The boy's body is to be rushed to New York within a few moments, so that specialists there can attend him, and on the way the attempts to resuscitate him will continue."

"Watch that ambulance!" Operator 5 ordered.

"I intend to do so. It is almost ready to leave. All arrangements have been made. Wait for a further report!"

Jimmy Christopher hung the receiver. His fingers strayed to the death charm on his watch-chain. Quietly he said: "Bring X-11 here, Chief. Bring him here at once!"

The Washington chief immediately spoke through the Dictaphone on the desk. A silent moment passed while they waited.

The door opened; an Intelligence man escorted X-11 into the room. The secret agent blinked in the light and passed a hand vaguely across his bandaged forehead. Z-7 stared incredibly as Jimmy Christopher gestured the living dead man into a chair.

Quietly Operator 5 asked: "Do you remember—remember when you died?"

The answer was a breath: "No!"

"Do you remember me?"

"I never—saw you before—tonight."

"You do not recall this office? Do you recall your designation?"

"I was—never here before. I don't know exactly what you mean by that."

"You," Jimmy Christopher asserted firmly, "are Intelligence Operator X-11."

The wounded man's eyes widened. "No. I am Three Hundred Twelve. That is my name—Three Hundred Twelve."

Z-7 stared appalled. Jimmy Christopher leaned closer. "Try to remember! Try to remember the Temple in the valley—the man in red. The Master of Death—"

"I know the Master of Death!" X-11 blurted. "I serve him!"

Operator 5 asked quietly: "You know that you once died? You know that the Master of Death brought you back to life?"

"Yes—yes, I know! I do not remember, but he told me and I believe him! That is why I serve him! He is the greatest power in the world! He is the coming King!"

Jimmy Christopher rose. At his gesture, X-11 was led from the office. When the door closed, Operator 5 faced Z-7 grimly.

"He can remember nothing, Chief, beyond the moment when the Master of Death returned him to life. He knows nothing but service to the Master. Because of that condition of general amnesia, the Master is able to make slaves of those he resurrects!"

Z-7 EJACULATED: "But you saw X-11 shot through the brain! You say he was instantly killed! Now it is possible that he could have been made to live again? You must have been

146

mistaken. The bullet that struck him could not have ended his life."

"I left X-11 dead!" Jimmy Christopher's voice quickened. "It means that Dr. Kalmar, like most skilled surgeons, is able to repair certain damages to the human organism and cause it to live again. Brain surgery can accomplish marvels. It is another technique which Dr. Kalmar has called to aid him in his diabolical plan."*

* AUTHOR'S NOTE: As Operator 5 states here, surgeons have achieved miraculous results in the field of brain surgery. In November, 1934, for instance, at the New York County Penitentiary, a prisoner, Joe Fatigate, age 25, was found after a fight among prisoners with the bone handle of a prison table-knife protruding from his forehead. The four-inch blade was buried in his brain. The prisoner did not lose consciousness. The blade of the knife broke off when two prison doctor's attempted to remove it. At a hospital, a surgeon used a strong pair of pliers to pull the blade out. The prisoner is at this writing apparently none the worse for his experience.

In 1932, during javelin practice at Bowdoin College, Tapping Selah Reeve, a freshman, was struck on the back of the head by a flying javelin and his skull was pierced. He pulled the spiked rod out and ran a quarter mile to the college infirmary. Tapping is now a junior with senior standing, president of the Chi Psi fraternity, and manager of the junior varsity football team.

At the Cleveland Clinic, two years ago, Dr. W. James Gardner removed the entire right half of a patient's brain in an attempt to cure her of attacks of epileptic fits. Four times previously surgeons had removed the right side of the brain from patients and each time it had proved fatal. Dr. Gardner's operation, however, succeeded. A few hours after the operation, the woman

"God! Is there no limit to that man's powers?"

"No limit," Operator 5 answered, "to the powers he hopes to achieve, Chief. You heard X-11 hail him as the coming King. The Master of Death plans to make himself the Monarch of the United States. He told me as much. He is exerting his force through many channels—and the most dangerous is the unthinking worship of the people. With his unholy godlike powers, the people will elevate him to a position of supreme command when he wishes it."

"Then his plan has been in operation for months, perhaps years!"

"Yes! He has planned with the utmost care, with unequaled daring. In his obsession for power, he dreams of the creation of a monarchy in the United States. Behind him, he will have the strength of a soulless people. But this plan is not for their benefit; it is utterly selfish. It is a quest for personal power—for private riches beyond measurement. He will achieve his purpose, Chief, unless we can break his hold on the people before it grows too strong."

"You suspected this from the beginning!" Z-7 exclaimed. "Thank God for your insight, Operator 5! Without you, we

recognized and talked with her friends; she improved rapidly and the epileptic condition was cured. She returned to normal life.

These are only a few of the amazing achievements of brain surgeons similar to that which enabled Operator X-11 to live again after being shot through the head.

would be falling helplessly into the power of the Master of Death even now—without knowing it!"

The door of the communications-room opened and again the chief-dispatcher called in: "Report for Operator 5. T-6 on the wire!"

Operator 5 lifted the telephone quickly. T-6's voice spoke, breathless with suppressed tension.

"Operator 5! I have followed the ambulance through traffic to Morrell's city home. Specialists were there waiting—one of them is Dr. Ernest Martin Chesterly, who has just landed from Europe. These men were sent away at once, by Morrell himself. I got that information direct from Chesterly as he was leaving—I posed as a reporter. That—wait!"

T-6's voice dropped. "I can see the Morrell house from here! Another ambulance has just drawn up to the door! It is colored red—it is decorated with a golden crown! The door of the house is opening. Four men are coming out, carrying a stretcher. The body of the boy is lying on it. They're putting the stretcher into the ambulance. They—"

"Follow that car!" Operator 5 snapped. "Keep it in sight!"

"It's drawing away now!" T-6 blurted. "I'll report as soon as possible!"

The connection broke. Operator 5 turned grimly from the telephone. His dark eyes blazed into Z-7's.

"The Master of Death is striking at a high mark! He is still operating openly and fearlessly! That man's daring is without limit! T-6 is on a trail that may lead us to him again, Chief—we can only hope he'll come through!"

JIMMY CHRISTOPHER jerked on his hat. He strode to the door as the telephone rang. Z-7, answering the summons, blurted an exclamation that stopped Operator 5. Looking up he declared huskily:

"Another pigeon has come to Loft C! The autogyro has moved farther out—it is now above the bay—but it still has not located the point from which the birds are being liberated. There is another message signed by the Master of Death and addressed to you!"

Operator 5 picked up the extension instrument. To the undercover agent on duty at Loft C he commanded sharply: "Repeat the message that just came in!"

The response came quickly: " 'To Operator 5. It pleases me to inform you that your young friend is my prisoner. Nothing can save him from destruction as *Yajna*. Nor can you escape everlasting death I have promised you. Prepare for eternity!' Signed, 'The Master of Death.'"

Operator 5 lowered the instrument, grimly. "Chief, radio the men in the autogyros! Tell them again that they must find the place from which those pigeons are being released. They must! It's our only chance, Chief—our only chance!"

Operator 5's jaw-muscles bunched hard; his fingers played upon his golden death-charm as he jerked open the door. He hastened out with firm stride, with grim, determined purpose....

THE DOOR of the white, stone house on upper Fifth Avenue opened at Operator 5's knock. The stern-faced manservant faced him forbiddingly. When Jimmy Christopher declared: "I must see Mr. Morrell at once!" the answer came flatly:

"Mr. Morrell is seeing no one!"

"No one else, perhaps," Operator 5 declared coldly, "but he is seeing me!"

He thrust through the entrance, pushing the manservant aside. He strode swiftly across a vestibule. He thrust open a heavy oak door and stepped into the quiet of a sumptuously furnished library. The manservant hastened after him frantically as he strode toward a richly carved desk in the center of the room. From the chair behind it, a man rose—a giant of a man with haggard face and grief-stricken eyes.

He was J. Pomeroy Morrell, upon whose decision the financial fate of nations had often rested.

Operator 5 shook off the manservant's hand at his arm. He drew the flat silver case from his pocket while Morrell stared. At the touch of the concealed spring, the metal leaf opened and the document framed inside was revealed to the financier's eyes. Morrell read the identification of Operator 5 signed by the President of the United States and his haunted gaze lifted.

"Yes—yes!" he said vaguely. "What do you want? Why are you here?"

"I must talk with you alone, Mr. Morrell," Jimmy Christopher announced.

At Morrell's gesture, the outraged manservant withdrew. The door closed upon the quiet room. In the midst of wealth— between walls hung with priceless old masters, among rare books of great worth—J. Pomeroy Morrell waited silently for Operator 5 to speak.

"I know," Jimmy Christopher said quietly, "that you are suffering. I will spare you all I can—but I must demand information. It is necessary to the salvation of this nation!"

"What—what do you wish to know?" Morrell asked guardedly.

"Where is your son's body?"

The great man winced. He answered huskily. "He is—here." His large hand gestured.

Gently Operator 5 contradicted him: "That is untrue. Your son's body is not here. It has been carried away. You have allowed it to be taken. You are waiting now—waiting and hoping—to receive word that your son has returned to life."

Morrell stared stricken. He burst out: "Good God! How do you know? How did you learn?"

"You have consigned his body to the Master of Death. He appealed to your grief, to your love for your son. He promised you that the boy will live again, and you grasped at that promise as a last hope. That is true, Mr. Morrell, is it not?"

The huge man trembled. "I—I cannot speak if it means that this will become known?"

"You are speaking to me in the strictest confidence, sir. You have my word of honor."

Morrell straightened. "Very well," he said huskily. "Yes—it is true!"

"You scarcely dare hope that the Master of Death will fulfill his promise to you, Mr. Morrell. I assure you that he possesses the power to fulfill it. He is able to resurrect your son—but that boy, if he returns to you, will remember nothing. He will not recognize you as his father. He will not know the lavish care you have spent upon him. He will become, if he rises from the dead, an abject slave of the man who resurrected him!"

"God! What are you saying?"

"I am preparing you for a heartbreaking shock. I am revealing to you the true purposes of the Master of Death. He proposed the resurrection of your son in payment of a reward, did he not?"

"Yes—yes! But—"

"How," Operator 5 demanded, "will you repay him for his seeming miracle?"

MORRELL STEADIED himself with difficulty. "You must understand that I—I am scarcely myself. What has happened seems like a frightful dream. I was stunned by Clifford's death. I could do nothing when the man who calls himself the Master of Death appeared before me—nothing but obey him. He ordered me to send the specialists away. He placed before me a legal document—a paper carefully drawn up which will stand the test in any court, by which—"

"Yes?" Operator 5's tone was very sympathetic.

"I signed it! I was in despair, clutching at a last forlorn hope. I put my signature to that paper because the reward he demanded is nothing to me compared with the life of my son. He asked, and I agreed, to give five million dollars—!"

Operator 5 stared dumbfounded.

"Five million dollars upon the return of my son alive! Another payment of five million dollars one year from that date. By the terms of the contract, I am bound to pay the same sum to the Master of Death every year Clifford remains alive. I am able to pay. I do not regret the bargain. But—he is my son! He must not become the slave of any man!"

Operator 5 spoke quietly. "Mr. Morrell, it is possible that the Master of Death can return your son to you with unimpaired mental faculties. I seriously doubt it. But I do know that he is striving for the complete rule of this nation—that he is a threat to the existence of this country. I demand from you, Mr. Morrell, information which will aid me to destroy that danger!"

"I—I will do what I can, but my first thoughts are naturally for my son. If giving you information means danger to him—"

"It will not. But I must know where the Master of Death has taken your son's body. I must know where the man is hiding. Where is he?"

"I can't tell you that!"

"Do you know?"

"No!"

Operator 5 stared incredulously. "You allowed him to take the body to an unknown place? You have no way of reaching him? You do not know where—?"

"I don't know! Before God, I do not!"

Jimmy Christopher stood with jaw squared, eyes blazing, peering into the lined face of the financier. Bitter hopelessness stung his heart. He turned slowly. Dread filled him as he left the house where life had been promised to the dead, where a vital trail to the Master of Death had ended in darkness....

CHAPTER 12
WAITING WINGS

OPERATOR 5'S eyes were dark with self-absorption when he entered the chief's inner office in secret Intelligence headquarters B-3. He found Z-7 listening intently to a message coming over the telephone line. The gray-clad man jerked up as Jimmy Christopher entered and snapped into the transmitter:

"Hold the line! Repeat that report again!" To Operator 5 he urged. "Take the other phone!"

Jimmy Christopher raised the receiver of the extension instrument and heard a breathless voice.

"This is L-2 reporting. I have just learned of T-6's death. He was struck down a few moments ago by a heavy automobile on Park Avenue. The men driving the machine scattered immediately, leaving T-6 pinned under it. He was killed instantly. The report just reached police headquarters and—"

"Try to trace that car!" Z-7 snapped. He clashed the receiver on its hook and peered at Jimmy Christopher. "That will come to nothing. I'm sure of it!"

Operator 5 rose grimly. "Another trail to the Master of Death has been destroyed! T-6 was following the red ambulance, and some of the Master's secret agents learned of it. They deliberately murdered him to clear the trail. Chief, every means of reaching Dr. Kalmar is being cut off from us. The radio cars of the police department—?"

"They have not located any of the automobiles used by Kalmar and his men to escape from the house on the Drive tonight," Z-7 admitted. "It is hopeless to look for a lead in that confusion. By this time, Dr. Kalmar is safely hidden and—"

"Our one remaining hope," Jimmy Christopher declared, "is the tracing of the carrier pigeons. We're still almost completely in the dark about the point from which they are liberated. That trail will vanish also if Dr. Kalmar ceases freeing the birds. There has been none since—?"

"Not while you were away from headquarters," Z-7 answered.

The jangle of the telephone bell turned Z-7 to the desk. He repeated "D-12—yes!" and gestured Jimmy Christopher to the extension.

"Following your orders, Chief," D-12 said, "I was detailed from WDC-13 to watch Major-General Rosson. He has just arrived in New York by plane. I followed as close as I dared, knowing that he is bringing with him a report on the state of national defenses. He is about to leave the airport—I've got to hurry if I'm to keep him in sight. I do not know his destination."

"Stick to him, D-12!" Z-7 commanded. "Report again as soon as you learn where he is going."

Operator 5 gazed at Z-7 thoughtfully as the connection broke. "General Rosson in New York—a report," he mused. "The President is in the city, Chief. He has come to his home here for the weekend. It may be that—" His voice died away as he rose.

There was silence in the office as Z-7 studied reports that had been placed on his desk. His gaze drifted from them. He asked slowly:

"Is it possible that the Master of Death can succeed in establishing a monarchy in the United States if he is not hindered? Will a free people submit to such a rule?"

"The Master of Death is taking advantage of a psychological quirk of the human mind, Chief. A people must have a ruler. The stronger he is, the more they admire him. Remember that there are hundreds of thousands in this country who have spent part of their lives under the rule of kings and dictators. In time of turmoil, such as we are experiencing now, the people not only submit to strict rule—they crave it! The path to a throne over the United States lies open to the Master of Death—if he can achieve it!"

Z-7 DEMANDED huskily: "In God's name—what can we do? You say our only lead is to trace the liberated carrier-pigeons. The men at Loft C are waiting for them now. They will report to this office the instant another bird appears. No report means that for the time being that trail is blocked. If Dr. Kalmar chooses not to release another bird—we're check-mated!"

Jimmy Christopher's fingers strayed to his death-charm; he sat lost in thought. For a long time he was motionless, gazing darkly into space. Dread drew deep lines around his eyes as he recalled the last message of the Master of Death—the message promising to make a human sacrifice of Tim Donovan.

Anxiety for the boy chilled Jimmy Christopher's heart. Since the night on the lower East Side, two years previous, when the rain-drenched and hungry urchin had saved Operator 5 from a gunman's bullet, they had grown dearer to each other than blood brothers. Now the threat of the Master of Death haunted Jimmy Christopher's mind more strongly with each passing moment.

He turned at last to face Z-7. "Chief, we are forced to wait, but—there is another chance. I have evolved a plan. It may not succeed, but it is at least a hope. We know the Master of Death is working rapidly now, striving to build up his mystic organization as strongly as possible—to spread it as far as possible. He works his spell under the cover of darkness. When night comes again he may once more gather his worshipers about him to preach his evil gospel. Gambling on that chance, Chief—"

Operator 5 came close to Z-7's desk. "I suggest that you withdraw all our men from their present details with the exception of D-12, who is shadowing Major-General Rosson. Issue new orders to them, directing them to learn if possible of any new meeting that is taking place tonight. Instruct them to be ready for concerted action should a meeting take place. We must summon all our strength to strike as heavily as possible if the chance comes."

Operator 5 went on: "In addition, order our agents from all surrounding cities, including Washington. Instruct them to come by plane and report immediately they arrive. Call every available man, Chief!"

Z-7 nodded, picked up the Dictaphone.

"The real chance, Chief—" Operator 5 spoke carefully. "Through the Federal Communications Commission, please connect at once with all the principal broadcasting stations in New York City. Arrange matters so that at any time of the day or night we may make use of all the stations together. We are to be allowed to interrupt any program we choose for a few minutes, to make a special announcement."

Jimmy Christopher seized Major-General Rosson's wrist!

Z-7 nodded again.

"Part of these plans, Chief," Jimmy Christopher continued, "must provide for the installation of microphones at the head-quarters-building at Mitchell Field, Long Island. The mikes are to be kept ready for use on short notice. I will not use these facilities if we succeed in locating the source of the carrier pigeons, but if we do not—"

Operator 5 paused as the telephone rang. Z-7 answered the summons and again signaled Jimmy Christopher to the extension instrument Operator D-12 spoke hurriedly:

"Chief, I have discovered Major-General Rosson's destination! It is the home of the President! He has just gone in and—"

Operator 5 snapped away from the 'phone. He jerked open the door of the Communications room and ordered the startled chief-dispatcher: "Get connection with the President's New York home—instantly. Connect him with Z-7!"

Under the imperative ring of Jimmy Christopher's voice, the hands of the man at the telephone switchboard flew from plug to socket. Operator 5 turned back as Z-7 rose in bewilderment. As he snatched up his hat and moved to the door he barked: "Urge the President not to see General Rosson until I join him!"

The closing door chopped off the words; Operator 5's swift heel-beats sounded beyond....

OPERATOR 5 swung his roadster to a stop in front of a house just west of Fifth Avenue, in midtown New York. He hurried to the door and rang. A Secret Service man opened it recognized him, allowed him to enter at once. He stepped into a quiet vestibule as two other men entered from a room beyond.

"General Rosson—?"

"Is here and waiting." The answer came from the President's first secretary. "We have followed instructions."

"Very well." Operator 5 peered at the second of the two. He was chief of the White House detail, whose duty was to protect the President. "You are to hold yourself ready for an emergency."

"Good Lord! An emergency—when the Chief of Staff is calling on the President?"

"Exactly!" Operator 5 gestured, and the secretary led him down a hallway. As they entered a quiet room, walled with bookshelves, a strong-faced man rose from his chair behind a desk. He smiled warmly and gripped Operator 5's hand.

"I am delighted to see you. What is all the excitement about?"

Jimmy Christopher answered: "I am here on a matter of the utmost importance. Before you see Major-General Rosson, I must speak to you privately."

At the gesture of the Chief Executive, the secretary and the chief of the White House detail withdrew. Behind closed doors Operator 5 faced the President. He asked quietly:

"Has Z-7 reported to you the facts of the case which is absorbing us?"

"In full," the President answered. "I have studied them carefully. They are the most amazing documents I have ever read!"

"You know, then," Jimmy Christopher continued, "that the Master of Death plans to usurp your position. You know that he schemes to destroy the office of President and establish himself as the ruler of this nation. He may do that by eliminating the office of President by constitutional amendment; or he may achieve the same result by transforming the President into a powerless figurehead—by making the Chief Executive a slave to obey his bidding!"

The President's face lost color. "Do you believe he will attempt—?"

"Nothing is beyond him, Mr. President! There is no move too daring for him to make. I cannot say more now about the danger you are facing. I can only warn you that the danger exists. If it is possible for me to remain in this room while Major-General Rosson is here—"

The President frowned. "Yes. You have only to step behind that screen. But Rosson! Why—?"

"I suggest, Mr. President," Operator 5 said as he rose, "that you call the Major-General into your study now."

HE STEPPED quietly behind the screen standing at one side of the room. He sensed a hesitation on the part of the Chief Executive; then, faintly, in a room beyond, a buzzer sounded. The secretary entered and left with instructions to bring the Chief of Staff in. Heavy footfalls neared; the door opened again. A man unseen to Operator 5 approached the desk of the President.

"My compliments, sir," came the chesty voice of Major-General Rosson. "I will take but little of your time. You requested me some time ago to prepare a report on the state of the defense of the nation. I have it ready."

The President hesitated again. "I do not recall asking you to prepare such a report, General. I have complete data on our defenses at my disposal constantly. There has been some mistake."

"Mistake?" Rosson echoed. "Perhaps—but you will receive the report in any case. I have it here in my briefcase. I will leave it with you."

Operator 5 eased soundlessly to the edge of the screen. He was behind Major-General Rosson; he could see the President clearly across the desk. The eyes of the Chief Executive were troubled. He watched the Chief of Staff open a bulky briefcase and reach inside it Major-General Rosson's hand lifted into the light and at that instant Jimmy Christopher leaped.

The screen spilled over as he readied desperately for die Chief of Staff's thick wrist. He seized it in white-corded fingers as a gasp of fury broke from Rosson. The President sprang to his feet in alarm during the swift, frantic struggle. Operator 5 jerked back, his face hard and cold—gripping the huge automatic that he had torn from the General's hand.

"Great Scott, Rosson!" the President ejaculated. "You're mad!"

The army officer stood recoiled against the desk, his face working with fury. The leveled gun in Operator 5's hand warned him to quietness while his muscles tensed for a savage leap. Breath beat hotly from his lungs; he stared fierce defiance as Jimmy Christopher straddled before him.

"You have brought unparalleled dishonor to the uniform you wear, Major-General Rosson!" Operator 5 grated.

The President's secretary and the chief of the White House Secret Service detail burst into the room. They stopped short in amazement, seeing the leveled gun in Jimmy Christopher's hand. He commanded: "Seize that man! He came here to kill the President!"

Rosson snarled, "That's not true!"

The President cautioned breathlessly, "If you are not absolutely sure of what you say—"

"I am certain beyond all doubt!" Operator 5 exclaimed. "Look into Rosson's briefcase. You will find no report such as he mentioned there. His 'report' was a ruse for gaining admission to you here, Mr. President. He came to kill you—under orders!"

Again the cornered man snarled defiance. Operator 5 straightened grimly. "Before you, Mr. President, stands a man who recently died. He was killed by contact with a high tension wire. He was resurrected by the Master of Death. So swiftly did the Master of Death work in this instance that Rosson reappeared, alive, before the world knew that he was dead. He was called back from death and made a slave of the man who revived him. He has acted under orders which he considers to come from a higher authority than you, Mr. President—orders from the Master of Death!"

MAJOR-GENERAL ROSSON straightened, his lips curling into a leer. "Very well," he growled. "I admit my higher command. I admit your charges. I demand to know what you will do with me for attempting to assassinate your Commander-in-Chief. You can do nothing which the Master of Death cannot undo with his power!"

"Not even the Master of Death," Jimmy Christopher declared coldly, "can bring you back a traitor life which the bullets of a firing squad have blasted away!"

The officer's huge face grew white. The President peered intently at Operator 5. "I am so stunned that I can scarcely think. I cannot express my gratitude to you. There is no doubt of what you say now. Rosson's intention—"

"Was to open the way to the Master of Death," Operator 5 continued. "You may be sure that the Master of Death is waiting even now to hear the news of your assassination. He realizes that your death would disrupt the country during this time of stress. He planned to intervene before the word was released to the world—to enter this house with his contrivances and to resurrect your dead body. Using all his skill as a surgeon, all his devices, he would bring life back to you."

"But—he would accomplish nothing if—"

"If he failed in your case, Mr. President, he would make the attempt again upon the man who would succeed to your office. If he succeeded, you would return to life with an impaired mind—with a mind subservient to his. He would order, and you would obey. You would become a figurehead, and he would become the executive. His power would then have been established—the end of the United States as a republic would have been very near!"

Major-General Rosson was staring at Operator 5 stolidly. "You have still not destroyed the Master's plans," he snarled. "My failure means nothing. He is immortal—his power is great enough to crush any who defy him!"

The President rounded the desk quickly. "Rosson," he declared sternly, "you are going to be held. Because of the grave condition of the country, I am going to let no word of this attempt reach the public."

Operator 5 laid the huge automatic on the President's desk

as the chief of the White House detail covered Rosson. "You are to see to it," he directed the Secret Service man, "that the precautions for protecting the President are doubled. Until the Master of Death is destroyed, the President will not be safe!"

Major-General Rosson strode heavily from the room in front of the gun. The President closed the door tightly. His hand sought Operator 5's, gripped it hard. "Operator 5—my gratitude!"

Jimmy Christopher smiled. "My gratitude, instead, sir, for the opportunity of stopping that madman's bullet. That is the appalling plan of the Master of Death—to make slaves of the leaders of our government, to wield his power through them. To make a vassal even of you, Mr. President!"

CHAPTER 13
BETWEEN TWO WORLDS

AT THE fifty-fourth floor of the Vertex Building, an elevator-cab slid to a stop. Through the opened grills, into the foyer of the offices masking secret Intelligence headquarters B-3, two men stepped. One was Operator M-10. The other was a portly man of dignified manner, with a short gray beard, whose eyes were blindfolded with a black handkerchief.

Operator M-10 led the unseeing man into an inner office. It contained only two chairs. Its walls shut away the sounds of the city. Once the door closed, M-10 removed the black band from the other man's eyes. In the light, the bearded man blinked with confusion.

"Wait here, please," M-10 directed.

He stepped out quickly. The other took a chair, his face mirroring his bewilderment. He waited through long, empty moments. At last a footfall sounded outside the door and it opened. Operator 5 strode into the room.

Jimmy Christopher extended his hand. "I consider it an honor," he said sincerely, "to meet you, Dr. Chesterly. Our precautions in bringing you here were necessary. We are engaged upon a vital and important task, and we need your cooperation. I am—"

Operator 5 displayed his credentials to Dr. Ernest Martin Chesterly. The famed scientist gazed his surprise. He said quietly: "I assure you I will aid you to the best of my ability."

Jimmy Christopher said: "Thank you! I know that you have just returned from Moscow, where you undertook a series of important experiments in resurrection with Dr. Brjuchenenko. You achieved amazing results which have not been revealed to the world. Your new knowledge is vital to us. You are the one man who can aid me more than any other to break the power of one who calls himself the Master of Death. Listen!"

Jimmy Christopher spoke rapidly. Dr. Chesterly heard him with mounting amazement, with deepening indignation. He said nothing until Operator 5 finished. Then, outraged, he blurted:

"Dr. Kalmar has dishonored science! He is making a ghastly mockery of the greatest achievement in our field. I will do everything possible to combat his evil work!"

"It is a dangerous task, Dr. Chesterly—dangerous beyond measure. It may cause your own death—your own destruction."

"I am not afraid of that!"

Operator 5 smiled tightly. "Thank God, you are willing to chance it! I suggest that you telephone your home and cancel all appointments for the remainder of the week, regardless of their importance. It will be necessary for you to stay here and wait. When the moment comes, we will call upon you."

"I will do it gladly!"

Again Jimmy Christopher gripped the firm, steady hand of the great scientist. He conducted Dr. Chesterly into another office, placed a telephone at his disposal, and withdrew, cautioning the surgeon that the utmost secrecy must be preserved. He strode then to the door of the Washington chief's office. Z-7 sprang up when he entered.

"I have been waiting for you to return! I have reports here—staggering reports! They show clearly the daring extent of the Master of Death's plan!"

JIMMY CHRISTOPHER took up the dispatches as Z-7 continued: "There is information on twenty men who hold highly important positions—each a slave of Dr. Kalmar! The Governors of three states! A member of the President's cabinet! Officers high in command in the Army and Navy! Men who control political factions! Ministers of the churches! The heads of police departments! God knows how many more men the Master of Death has enslaved that we do not know about yet!"

Operator 5, scanning the reports, noted that each of the men named was clearly suffering from strange attacks resembling amnesia; that their characters had undergone striking changes; that their attitudes in office had become disruptive and dangerous. He returned the reports to Z-7's desk grimly.

"Exactly as I expected, Chief! The Master of Death has been working a long time. His plan is to continue until he has assumed control of all our key-men. We must destroy him before that plan reaches any farther. It is still possible to remove these men from their offices—but we dare not allow this devilish work to continue!"

Z-7's fingers twined together. "God!" What can we do? We are still waiting—waiting for another pigeon to return to Loft C—and none appears! It is our only possible chance of locating Dr. Kalmar—and the way is blocked!"

Jimmy Christopher turned to the telephone. He called a number; he asked quietly of the Intelligence operator who answered: "You are still questioning Major-General Rosson? Have you been able to get any information from him?"

"Nothing! He does not know where the Master of Death is hiding. It's impossible to learn that through him."

Jimmy Christopher disconnected; again he called a number—Loft C. When the answer came, he demanded: "No other pigeon has returned?"

"No, sir! No sign of one!"

Operator 5 turned slowly from the instrument. Again his fingers toyed with his golden death-charm as he peered at the twirling red second-hand of the electric clock. Precious hours had passed. A torturously long day had crept by. Night had come again—a night which promised to be empty of all leads to the Master of Death. Jimmy Christopher rose tensely, his lips pressed hard.

"Lord, Chief! Thinking of Tim—it's getting me. God knows what Dr. Kalmar has done to him by now. He may—he may already—"

He broke off, quickly taking up his hat. He demanded of Z-7: "Our men are waiting? We have every available agent on watch and ready to act? You can reach them immediately, if the chance comes?"

"Yes!" Z-7's voice was full of sympathy.

"Then we can wait no longer! I must try to force the Master of Death into betraying himself. It's a thousand-to-one gamble, but there's no other way. Chief—come with me!"

Z-7 hurried after him into the corridor. To the agent who was standing outside the door of the room in which Dr. Chesterly was waiting. Operator 5 said quietly:

"When orders to act come in, Dr. Chesterly is to follow with our men. He is to be guarded with the utmost care on the way. If our opportunity comes, his assistance will be absolutely vital."

"Yes, sir!"

They strode through the foyer of the offices; they descended in the elevator to the lobby of the great building. Operator 5 hurried to his roadster. Inside it, Diane Elliot and John Christopher were waiting. They had come with him from Address Y after he had returned there from the President's home. He quietly bade them to follow, and they turned to Z-7's sedan. The Washington chief took the wheel and asked quietly: "Where?"

"Mitchell Field!"

THE HEAVY car ran along the unpaved road on Long Island and turned to the barred entrance of Mitchell Field. Z-7 spoke quickly to the sentry on duty; the way was opened. The sedan rolled onto the spacious tarmac, into the lights gleaming from the windows of the operations-buildings and the barracks.

In the center of the field, in accordance with Operator 5's orders, an autogyro stood. Its weird vanes drooped; its muffled motor was idling. It was waiting to relieve the second craft which was then on duty in the air above New York Bay. Jimmy Christopher gazed at it intently as he strode with Z-7 and John Christopher and Diane Elliot toward the door of the Commanding Officer's headquarters, littered with air-charts.

A grave-faced Major greeted the Washington chief and Operator 5. Jimmy Christopher asked quietly:

"Have the microphones been installed? They are ready for use, Major Rankin?"

"They are ready." The Commanding Officer led the way into an adjoining room. There, on a desk, sat six microphones marked with the call letters of the major broadcasting stations in and around New York City. In the room, six control-boards had been brought; technicians were waiting near them. Operator 5 glanced at his watch. He strode to a desk in the corner of the room.

Again he called the number of Loft C. Again he anxiously demanded of the secret agent on duty there: "No pigeon has yet returned since last night?"

"No, sir!"

Grim-faced, Operator 5 turned to Z-7. "Chief, we must take

the gamble. It may not work, but—we can do nothing else!" He strode to the table, while the others in the room eyed him anxiously. The dark lines of his face had grown deeper. The glitter of his eyes had brightened. He sat before the microphones and brought them close. Crisply, he commanded the technicians at the control-boards:

"Clear the lines; I am going on the air at once!"

The monitors affixed ear-phones and thrust plugs into the sockets on the panels. They spoke quickly into the transmitter units. Major Rankin, opening a door, strode into the adjoining office and clicked the switch of a small radio sitting on the desk. As the tubes warmed, Z-7 joined him and the sound of music issued into the room.

Almost immediately, the melody faded away. The voice of an announcer spoke quickly:

"Ladies and gentlemen of the radio audience, we interrupt the program for an important announcement. Please stand by!"

There was a pause. Z-7 closed the connecting door as the technicians at the monitor boards signaled their readiness to Operator 5 at the table. Out of the radio then—flashing by wire to the major broadcasting stations, traveling back like invisible lightning through the ether—Jimmy Christopher's voice issued:

"Operator 5 is speaking. I am calling the man known as the Master of Death!"

Z-7 listened with cold apprehension. He realized that nothing save the gravest emergency would force Jimmy Christopher to even partially reveal himself. He knew that millions of radios scattered around the metropolis were reproducing Operator 5's voice. The startling announcement continued in Jimmy Christopher's firm tones:

"Operator 5 is calling the Master of Death! I have received your warning. I accept your challenge! I defy you with a promise to reveal your evil mockery to the people. I swear that I will disclose to them the fact that you possess no mystic powers, that the results you achieve can be attained by any physician in possession of your devices and your technique. I declare that I will tear your false cloak of power from you!"

JIMMY CHRISTOPHER'S voice rose and rang:

"You and I face each other now in a battle to an everlasting end!"

Silence again. Z-7 turned from the radio, opened the communicating door, and peered at Jimmy Christopher. He was gesturing to the technicians, rising from the chair. They were pressing signal-buttons on their monitor-boards. Amazement shone in every face.

The faint strains of music returned to the adjoining office as Operator 5 hurried to the outer door. John Christopher, with a frantic movement, caught at his arm and stopped him. Ex-Operator Q-6 blurted:

"Good God, son, what have you done?"

Jimmy Christopher declared tightly: "I have laid a trap for the Master of Death!" He turned quickly to Z-7. "Chief, I'm taking the autogyro. I'm going to relieve the craft that is now on duty. I'm going to assume the watch myself. I pray that the Master of Death—"

He broke off, tight-lipped, and strode out the door. John

Christopher, stricken pale, hurried after him. Z-7 and Diane Elliot followed with Major Rankin. Operator 5, striding to the waiting autogyro, commanded crisply to the pilot:

"We're taking off at once!"

Again John Christopher seized his son's arm. "You are taking a desperate chance! You are risking Tim's life! You can't do this, Jimmy—you can't!"

"I'm doing it because nothing else is possible, Dad!" Operator 5 answered firmly. He stepped closer. "You are concerned for Tim and me, I know—yet that is not the real reason why you are trying to stop me!"

John Christopher stared. "Jimmy, what do you mean? I will not allow you to carry through your challenge to the Master! I forbid you—!"

Operator 5's sharp eyes stifled his father's voice. "I am seeing it through, Dad! Try to take hold of yourself! You want to keep me back because you want no harm to befall the Master of Death. You are facing death constantly—you do not want your fear of it to return. You look upon the Master of Death as a savior when he is actually an annihilator. His spell has been growing on you, hour by hour. In spite of what I have warned you, you would become his slave at his merest word!"

John Christopher stood rigid. "Jimmy, I implore you not to attack that man! I beseech you not to take from me the hope of—"

"You can't stop me, Dad! Not even you can stop me!"

Operator 5 turned away grimly; he gripped the cowling of the autogyro. As he lifted himself, John Christopher started forward desperately. Ex-Operator Q-6 grasped his son's shoulders; frantically he dragged Operator 5 back. In terror he clung—until Jimmy Christopher tore free.

"Dad!" Jimmy Christopher's face darkened with agony. "Dad—you are under arrest!"

John Christopher echoed in dismay:

"Under—?"

"Under arrest!" Operator 5 gestured sharply to the appalled Z-7. "Take him into custody, chief! Hold him! That man is my prisoner!"

JIMMY CHRISTOPHER was pale as a ghost as he gripped the cowling of the gyro again. His father started forward desperately; Z-7 stepped alertly to block the way. Major Rankin seized the arms of Ex-Operator Q-6 and held him back. Tears streamed from the old man's eyes as he struggled to free himself, as he watched his son climb into the pit.

"Take off!" the command rang.

The motor of the plane rose to a roar. Jimmy Christopher's hands closed white on the cowling as he peered into his father's wretched eyes. In the tearing slipstream, Diane Elliot started forward, her eyes wide, her red lips parted.

"Jimmy! Jimmy, I understand!" she shouted. "See it through! Good luck—good luck!"

Operator 5's throat grew chokingly tight as the brakes went free of the landing trucks, as the gyro began to roll. Wind tore past him as it gathered speed. It trundled through the shafting lights while its weird vanes spun. Suddenly it left the ground, climbing at a steep angle. It swerved up into the darkness and

Operator 5 peered down at the white faces of the men and the girl watching him....

The lights of the field sank into the deep night. The autogyro swooped toward the shore-line—toward the black waters of the bay. In its rear pit, Operator 5 watched until the gleam of Mitchell Field vanished in a bewildering pattern of lights. He waited grimly as the muffled motor of the gyro carried him out into the blackness of sky and water....

The shine of Manhattan faded into the background. Below twinkled the lights of ferries and tugs, of an ocean steamer being piloted into the harbor. Even these spots dimmed as Operator 5 was carried farther away from the towered city. He brought binoculars from a pocket in the cubby; he scanned the sky ahead until he glimpsed a lightless black form hovering in the night.

Straight toward the other patrolling gyro, Jimmy Christopher flew. He swerved close as it circled. Immediately the other craft swerved away, the observer pointing straight out to sea. Jimmy Christopher checked the direction on the compass; he signaled his pilot into position. While the first craft faded off into the vastness of the night, he assumed the gambling vigil.

He pressed binoculars to his eyes and peered out into the darkness. Never lowering the lenses a moment, he ordered his pilot around in a tight circle. The darkness was intense; the sea lay black under a black sky. The baffling gloom brought a heavy sense of hopelessness to Operator 5's heart. He continued to search the air, sweeping his circle of vision, while endless minutes trailed past....

Again and again the gyro weaved up and down and through

its circle. The pilot played his controls tensely. The great bat hovered in an unworldly hush. Deep rings became stamped around Operator 5's eyes while he continued to press the glasses close. Minute after minute—each an eternity—minute after minute....

Operator 5 tensed. The swinging circles of his vision caught in the air a flutter so faint that he was not sure he had seen it at all. It appeared only to vanish instantly. Swiftly Jimmy Christopher swept his binoculars in a desperate attempt to find it again in the black air. A dark glisten reappeared for a fraction of a second. A jerk, and he again caught it. Through the powerful lenses he followed the sweep of speeding wings! A pigeon!

It was flying out of the darkness blanketing the sea, toward the shine of the city lights beyond. Operator 5, for one instant, discerned a bright metal tube affixed to one of its slender legs. A message! He smiled tightly—a wry smile of triumph. The Master of Death had heard his radioed challenge and was answering it!

Quickly Operator 5 shouted orders that sent the gyro speeding farther out to sea. He watched the compass intently; he made certain that the needle did not waver. Overhead, the vanes spun; the muffled motor whispered; the strange craft followed a line straight as an arrow into the recesses of the night. From somewhere out in that sea of darkness, the pigeon had been liberated. Somewhere in that baffling gloom, lieutenants of the Master of Death had released it....

THE GYRO followed a direction which lay at an angle from the previous approach of the patrolling craft. It coursed swiftly.

177

Jimmy Christopher played his lenses downward, tensed again as a sparkle of light came out of the night.

His orders sent the gyro into a climb. It soared high while it swept toward the lights. They grew brighter steadily. Operator 5 discerned the beacons of a ship. Its ports were shafting bright beams. Its decks were a-shine. Its funnels were pouring smoke. Yet it was scarcely moving on the dark sea. Drifting on smooth water, the ship lay remote from all others—remote from everything save the autogyro that whispered toward it.

Jimmy Christopher signaled his pilot again, and the craft dropped low. It swung close to the surface beyond the shine of the lights. Operator 5 peered through his glasses grimly, sweeping the length of the vessel. The circles of his vision paused at its bow. The ship carried no name. Instead, it bore an insignia—a symbol of gold against a red background. The royal crown!

Operator 5's snapped command sent the gyro soaring. He quickly clicked the switch of the radio equipment. His eyes blazed as he affixed ear-phones and brought a microphone close. His heart speeded with a cold hope while he waited for the tubes to heat. A hiss sounded in the 'phones. Operator 5 checked the oscillator, and the transmitter carried his ringing voice. "Calling B-3! Calling Z-7 at B-3!"

Immediately an answer flashed back. "B-3 picking you up! All clear, Operator 5! Z-7 has just come into the office! He's—"

The voice of the Washington chief broke in. "Yes, Operator 5! Have you orders?"

"Orders, Chief! The Master of Death took the bait and answered my challenge. I spotted the carrier pigeon. It was released from a ship which has been constantly changing course! It is below me now—a vessel of the Master! Note its position!"

Rapidly Operator 5 checked his instruments; he snapped into the transmitter the approximate location of the steamer which lay below. Z-7 answered tightly:

"I have it, my boy! I have just received reports from our operators stationed along the waterfront. They inform me that many small boats are putting out—power-launches, chartered ferries, small steamers! Hundreds of people are boarding them! It means that another meeting of the Master is assembling tonight aboard the vessel you have found!"

"Exactly! Flash orders at once! Call in every Coast Guard boat near New York! Order amphibian planes broken out! Commandeer any small craft you can find! Order our men to proceed as quickly as possible to the ship I have found! They are to approach close and board it when they see me reach it!

"Order at least twenty of our best men to take off in airplanes and to drop to the deck of the ship by parachute immediately after me! Once the way is open, the others are to come aboard. Dr. Chesterly is to be brought by one of the boats. It must be a concerted surprise action. This time, chief, we can cut off all avenues of escape for Dr. Kalmar and his men!"

Jimmy Christopher raised from the microphone. He peered again, grimly, coldly, at the vessel riding the water below—the ship of the Golden Crown, drifting between two worlds!

CHAPTER 14
RETREAT OF DEATH

HIGH IN the black sky hovered the autogyro carrying Jimmy Christopher. Anxiety weighted his heart during the enforced period of waiting. He peered down at the sea through his binoculars—and out of the darkness of the waters he saw the lights of small craft appear.

They came swarming out of the bay—launches, ferries, coastwise craft. Through his lenses, Operator 5 discerned that their decks were crowded with men and women. Suspended in the sky, he watched the craft approach the ship of the Golden Crown. He saw accommodation ladders lowered from four points of the great ship's deck; he watched the small boats pull alongside....

Men and women thronged up the ladders. On the deck, lieutenants of the Master of Death directed the gathering congregation toward the companionways. A steady stream of humans poured across the deck, from the ladders, to disappear below. Immediately the small boats were emptied, they shuttled away and others darted close. Again and again their passengers crowded up, driven by a mystic hope. One after another, other smaller boats appeared, unloaded, and withdrew. The forces of the Master of Death were gathering!

Soon the water around the ship of the Golden Crown became clear. Again Operator 5 was forced to wait for a torturous period. Steadily the gyro hovered over its position. Now the decks of the great ship were uncrowded; the hundreds who had boarded her were all below, save for a few men standing guard at the heads of the accommodation ladders. And into the air, through the whisper of the varied craft's motor, rose the sound of a swelling voice—the chant of the worshipers of the Master of Death....

Jimmy Christopher tightened when he saw the vague shapes of other boats approaching from the bay. He discerned the lines of Coast Guard cutters, of others flocking with them. As their beacons twinkled in the distance, he swung to a position directly above the steamer of the Golden Crown. He saw the lights of the approaching craft wink out. In deep darkness they approached their mark, bearing determined men of the Intelligence service.

Then into the sky came the drone of motors. Operator 5 swung his glasses to see amphibian planes winging out of the night sky. Driving from the direction of Mitchell Field, they came swarming. Quickly Jimmy Christopher trimmed the oscillator of the radio transmitter to the wavelength used by those planes. His voice rang orders again: "Circle above the ship! Bail out as soon as you see me drop! Ready!"

The approaching planes swept into a high circle. As they banked, Jimmy Christopher drew the pack of a parachute from beneath the cubby seat. He buckled it about him. Gripping the cowling, he rose. His pilot watched alertly, obeying his signals. He climbed over and hung. He gazed at the great ship directly below—and dropped!

Plummeting through black air, he jerked at the rip-cord of the pack. The pilot 'chute flicked out; the great silken bell blossomed. Red light reflected on it from the ship below as Operator 5 pendulumed. Gripping the shroud-lines, he spilled air from the silk, directing himself toward the deck of the Golden Crown vessel as he sank….

Below him the deck spread. The sentries at the ladder-platforms were staring warily into the sky, alarmed by the noise of the motors. Operator 5 peered up as he swung, and saw white spots against the night sky—many floating parachutes! The Intelligence men brought by the planes had bailed out. In the air a constellation of silken stars glimmered—twenty! Downward out of the night came the first attack…!

JIMMY CHRISTOPHER pulled the shrouds again, directing himself toward the open after-deck. The red gleam of the ship lights shone on him brightly now. He saw men wearing armbands running—running toward the spot where he would alight. His hand slipped his automatic out. He leveled it and before his feet touched the deck his sharp command rang: "Back! Keep back or be destroyed!"

Destroyed! The deadly word brought a momentary halt to the approaching men. They gripped guns, but they did not fire. Jimmy Christopher's weapon waved from one to another of them as he floated to the deck. He straddled to keep upright and swiftly loosened the buckles of the harness. The rolling 'chute tugged the straps off his shoulders as he shrugged out of the leather straps.

The lieutenants of the Master of Death started forward with a rush. A sharp cry from another section of the deck startled them. "Look up!" They stared into the air to see the other parachutes clustering in the air above. Downward to the deck of the ship twenty armed men were being carried on gossamer silk. Forward, the first of the men landed and struggled from the bellying chute. Others followed swiftly. As the wearers of the crimson arm-hands began to scatter, Jimmy Christopher darted along the rail.

The first Intelligence men sprang across the deck.

They crowded upon the Master of Death's lieutenants. Already they outnumbered the sentries. No gun was fired during the swift advance that forced the men with arm-bands to the rail. Service automatics menaced them constantly. They retreated, their stares defiant, as the Intelligence men surrounded them.

Operator 5 stood back while the lieutenants of the Master of Death were disarmed. They gave up their weapons with contemptuous willingness, as though they feared no danger. Jimmy Christopher, watching from the shadowed deck, heard the planes droning away overhead, saw the first outlines of approaching boats appear. From all around, Coast Guard cutters were nearing with other craft swarming beside them. The men aboard the boats had seen the parachutes land; they were sweeping across the sea swiftly.

Operator 5 hurried to a platform as the craft swung alongside. Other Intelligence men hurried up the ladders. Leading them, Z-7 came with an automatic gripped tightly in his hand. Jimmy Christopher stood with the chief at his side while the boats approached and discharged their men. They gathered silently on the after-deck, their faces grim. Among them, bewildered but unafraid, stood Dr. Chesterly.

"Careful!" Operator 5 warned. "We're going below. You are to hold the congregation back from the platform. Dr. Kalmar and

In cold fury, Operator 5 raced across the platform to where

the giant Karant was holding Tim Donovan lifeless!

his men are to be forced off. Stifle every show of opposition! We are to take absolute command of this meeting. Use your guns if necessary but remember—"

From below sounded the deep-throated tone of a gong. It struck again, a third time. As the reverberations melted away into the silence of the sea, an awesome voice rose—the chant of the worshipers of the Master of Death. It swelled in volume, hauntingly, ringing like a lament, yet vibrant with hope.

Operator 5 turned, grimly signaling his men after them. They trod quietly to the companionways. At his signal, they started down. The unified voice rose higher in its barbaric chant when they reached a foyer below. They approached a great arch which opened into a vast space beyond—a space filled with crimson light, a floating Temple of the Crown!

Its walls were the color of blood. It was as wide as the ship and almost as long—a cavernous meeting-place especially constructed. Pews filled it, and hundreds of men and women faced the raised platform at one end. Behind the platform fluttered a scarlet curtain. In front of it, two figures were visible—and sight of them brought a sharp chill to Operator 5's heart.

The tall, box-shouldered man was the living corpse who called himself Karant. He was holding a small figure before him—a figure suspended by the great hands that clutched about its neck. A boy! Tim Donovan!

OPERATOR 5 commanded sharply: "In!" He sped to the foot of the aisle that led between the pews; and his men followed. They darted to the flanks of the congregation, hurrying to surround the pews. Their move was swift; at first it was scarcely noticed by the fascinated congregation. As their lines lengthened, as they turned grimly to train their guns on the worshipers, a cry of consternation rose. Operator 5, rushing down the aisle toward the platform, whirled to shout: "Silence! Remain in your places and you will not be harmed! If you attempt to oppose us, you will be destroyed!"

Again the dread word shocked horror into those who heard it. Operator 5 whirled again to the platform to see men wearing scarlet arm-bands hurrying through the swinging crimson curtain. The secret agents following him sprang up, their guns threatening. Three shots blasted from the guns of the Master's lieutenants; a crackling fusillade answered. Two wearers of the arm-bands dropped, an Intelligence man staggered on a wounded leg. Jimmy Christopher sprang upon the dais and again shouted a command:

"Drop your guns. Drop them or be destroyed!"

The terror of the word stilled the attack as Operator 5 turned grimly to the center of the platform. There the huge man called Karant had not moved. He was still straddled, his great arms straining crushing fingers upon Tim Donovan's neck. The boy was dangling. Karant's wrists showed evidence of the desperate efforts Tim Donovan had made to tear himself free, but now his arms were hanging loose. His eyes were closed. His face was lax. His open mouth did not breathe.

Operator 5 drove a swift, hard blow to the side of Karant's head. The big man staggered under its power. Tim Donovan dropped limply to the floor as Karant whirled back. In cold fury Jimmy Christopher followed, driving blow after blow to the gaunt face of the living corpse. The glazed eyes rolled; Karant dropped backward, rolled, and lay still—unconscious.

Operator 5 spun back to Tim Donovan. The boy was lying limp on the platform. Eyes still closed, mouth open as though gasping for breath, he lay without moving. Jimmy Christopher knelt over him. He shook the boy's shoulders frantically.

"Tim! Tim!"

There was no response—no slightest response…. Operator 5 was unconscious of the turmoil around him. He did not know that the Intelligence men stationed around the floating Temple were forcing the fearful congregation back into their seats. He scarcely heard Z-7's voice ringing out into the hubbub of the crowd.

"Stay where you are! We have no intention of harming you! You are in no danger from us! Silence! Be silent!"

Desperately Operator 5 shook Tim Donovan again. The swollen whiteness of the boy's face struck him cold. The cruel bruises on the boy's neck, where Karant's fingers had crushed, filled him with a choking fury. He jerked up; his gaunt gaze swept the platform. At the rear the crimson curtain was fluttering. Red hands were appearing through it….

Out of the scarlet drapes stepped a figure robed in red, hooded in red, gloved in red. The Master of Death moved forward glidingly, with contemptuous disregard of the guns trained on him. His gesture checked the advance of those lieutenants who came after him from the curtained space behind the platform. He peered into Operator 5's pale face and spoke with a gloating ring:

"You have come too late. He is *Yajna!*"

JIMMY CHRISTOPHER'S aching eyes turned again to Tim Donovan's still form. Z-7 stepped close and gripped his arm. He spoke huskily, scarcely hearing his own words: "He's dead!… Dead!…"

Operator 5 stood motionless, unable to turn his eyes from the body of the boy who had been his friend….

Z-7's black eyes smoldered as he strode across the dais. To his men he commanded sharply: "Hold Dr. Kalmar! Keep all his men away! In God's name—where is Dr. Chesterly?"

Jimmy Christopher jerked back to realization of his surroundings as he heard the sound of the man. White-faced, he peered toward a movement in the temple. Through the reddened air, an anxious answer came: "I am here! I am coming!"

Down the aisle between the pews hurried the bearded scientist. While Dr. Chesterly climbed to the platform, Operator 5 peered furiously at the red figure of the Master of Death. He strode close; snatched at the red hood. He tore it away and glared burningly into Dr. Anton Kalmar's face.

"You are pale, Doctor! You are afraid! You feel your power slipping from you!"

He turned back as Dr. Chesterly bent over Tim Donovan's limp figure. The scientist felt for the boy's pulse. He rose, his manner calm, his eyes gleaming with a desperate hope. "The boy is dead. Yet he has been dead only a few moments. There is yet time…."

"For God's sake—hurry!"

Jimmy Christopher strode swiftly across the dais to the red curtains. He gripped them in hard fists. He tore them downward. The silk ripped from its supporting rings, baring the space beyond. Under bright lights, at the rear of the platform, sat the strange contrivances used in the resurrection of the dead.

Operator 5 strode in. At one side of the space, a litter was lying. Stretched beneath a crimson shroud that was marked with the golden crown was a boy. He was gazing at Jimmy Christopher weakly; he was breathing. He was J. Pomeroy Morrell's son.

Dr. Chesterly bustled among the apparatus after Operator 5. His glance swept the devices; he strode to the shelves at one wall which were loaded with bottles of reagents. He read the labels hastily. He turned to command imperatively: "Bring the boy! Bring him!"

Jimmy Christopher hurried to Tim Donovan. He raised the Irish lad in his arms. He carried Tim to Dr. Chesterly, who had turned to the teeter-board. The scientist had jerked off his coat and rolled up his sleeves. He leveled the board rapidly. With Jimmy Christopher's help, he placed Tim Donovan upon it.

"The straps! Quick!"

Each move swift and sure, the scientist and Operator 5 drew the buckles tight, fastening Tim Donovan immovably to the board. At Dr. Chesterly's command, two Intelligence operators hurried forward. They took positions beside the board at his gesture. He ordered them quickly: "Tilt it up and down! Head down, feet up, then the reverse! One! Two! One! Two! Continue that!"

The scientist turned immediately to a heavy compressor tank standing at one side. Jimmy Christopher rolled it closer. To its valves were attached rubber hoses which passed through bellows arrangements and connected with a cone-shaped aspirator. Dr. Chester pressed the device hurriedly upon Tim Donovan's white face as the boy's body was tilted with a regular rhythm. He strapped it in place as Jimmy Christopher opened the valves, and compressed air began to actuate the breathing bellows. While Tim Donovan's body was swung, head up, head down, his chest expanded and relaxed under, the pressure of the artificial lungs....

OPERATOR 5'S gaze followed Dr. Chesterly to the shelves. The scientist quickly opened several small bottles. He removed a hypodermic syringe from its case, sterilized a needle in an alcohol flame, and quickly filled the barrel of the device. He returned rapidly to the side of the teeter-board. "Stop—one instant only!"

The scientist bent over the lax body as the teeter-board went level and paused. The needle of the syringe plunged home. Its contents were discharged under pressure of Dr. Chesterly's thumb. The scientist stepped back and at his gesture the tilting was resumed....

Operator 5 peered across the dais. Z-7 was standing close, watching with hypnotic fascination. The Intelligence operators were ringed around the Temple, their guns leveled. The eyes of those who had come to worship the Master of Death were fixed upon the swinging teeter-board. Silence had come into the Temple. Upon the platform, held back by the guns of the secret agents, Dr. Kalmar and his assistants watched Dr. Chesterly work in cold fury....

Again the scientist turned to the shelves. Operator 5 sped to his side to assist him. When a second syringe was filled, they turned again to the teeter-board. Once more the steady swinging stopped. Once more a sharp needle sent the contents of the syringe into the veins of the boy who had been strangled in Karant's hard hands. Immediately the tilting of the board was resumed—and Operator 5 backed away anxiously.

A third time the scientist made an injection into Tim Donovan's body, while silence filled the Temple. When he withdrew, he turned grave eyes upon Jimmy Christopher. He said huskily, his head wagging:

"We have now done everything possible. Unless Dr. Kalmar is in possession of some secret which I—"

Jimmy Christopher swiftly strode to the loaded shelves; his gaze turned from bottle to bottle. Tightness came to his lips as he grasped the neck of one containing a viscid golden fluid. He turned away to see Dr. Kalmar starting forward under a mad impulse—a move that was blocked by the guns in the hands of the Intelligence man. Operator 5 carried the bottle of precious elixir to Dr. Chesterly.

"This is Dr. Kalmar's secret!"

Dr. Chesterly took the bottle eagerly. He removed its cork and smelled of its contents; he peered intently at its color. New light shone in his eyes as he strode again to the laboratory table. This time he took from a case a hypodermic syringe larger than the others. He fitted a long, strong needle to it. He filled the glass barrel with the glittering, golden fluid.

Swiftly he returned to the teeter-board. Operator 5 pressed close to his side as the up-and-down movements ceased. Dr. Chesterly gestured, and Jimmy Christopher ripped open Tim

Donovan's shirt. The scientist brought the long needle to the bare skin of the boy's chest—and paused.

"It is a risk," he said huskily. His eyes raised beseechingly to Dr. Kalmar's livid face. He demanded: "Sir, in the name of science, in the name of human mercy, I call upon you to inform me of the proper use of this extract."

Dr. Kalmar's answer thundered: "No! No!"

Jimmy Christopher turned tensely to Dr. Chesterly. "He will not speak. Trying to force him will only lose precious time. Take the chance, doctor—now!"

The scientist hesitated no longer. He ordered the teeterboard steadied. His nerveless hands brought the gleaming needle vertical over Tim Donovan's chest. Operator 5 stared in cold fascination as it plunged home. He watched while, drop by drop, the vital golden fluid was forced down the barrel. He heard Dr. Chesterly whisper: "The right ventricle of the heart…! The right ventricle!"

THE SCIENTIST withdrew the needle. Immediately the motion of the teeterboard was resumed. Tim Donovan's head was raised and lowered with steady rhythm. His chest rose and fell under the power of the compressed-air aspirator. Jimmy Christopher peered at Dr. Kalmar to see maniacal wrath flooding it. He turned quickly as an exclamation broke through Dr. Chesterly's lips.

The scientist was holding Tim Donovan's wrist, his fingers pressed to the artery. His eyes were agleam. He declared in a whisper:

"There is a pulse! It is strengthening! His heart is beating!"

193

A sob broke through Operator 5's lips. He peered into Tim Donovan's face and saw color returning to the skin. The eyelids of the boy were fluttering. Still the teeter-board swung up and down, up and down. Filled with cold, unflinching determination, Jimmy Christopher turned to face the assembly in the Temple of the Crown. He flung his bands high and his voice rang through the red air:

"Hear me! Look at the boy you saw sacrificed to a human monster! He was murdered by the man who—calls himself the Master of Death—killed without need! He was a sacrifice to powers which do not exist. The Master of Death has made the claim that he alone can bring the dead back to life, but you see his words being proven a lie!"

Out of the temple came a startled, angry muttering as Jimmy Christopher continued:

"Over and over again the Master of Death has deluded you! He has kept for himself, for his own evil purposes, a discovery which belongs to the world—a discovery which will be granted to humanity without any man or woman becoming Dr. Kalmar's slave! His discovery is real, but his mystic powers are false!"

Behind Operator 5, the teeter-board had been rising and falling. At its side, Dr. Chesterly continued to feel Tim Donovan's pulse. Now the scientist gave a gruff command. The swinging board stopped. The two secret agents loosened the straps. They caught the boy as he slid downward: they supported him.

His eyes were open—open and gazing out into the scarlet air of the temple. They were dimmed but living. He was breathing now without the aid of the artificial lung. He had been dead and now he was alive!

Through his aching throat Operator 5 cried: "You see it accomplished before you, without secrecy! You see science and science alone return the dead to life! He was dead and now he lives!"

From the temple, a startled shout echoed. "He lives!" It was taken up instantly: "He lives!" It rose like a cry of protest. There was no rhythm of the chant in it now. It voiced the rebellion of hundreds who, by the revelation Operator 5 had made, returned to reality.

"He lives!" From their seats the hundreds sprang. As though in contemptuous recoil from the false powers of the Master of Death, they fled up the aisles toward the arch. Their rush pushed back the Intelligence men. The strength of their numbers overwhelmed the armed agents. They mobbed to the curtained exit of the temple in a concerted rush.

Z-7's cry sounded shrill in the burst of pandemonium. "Watch Kalmar!"

AT THE first uproar, the man in the red robe had whirled back to the wall. A gun spat as he darted aside; the bullet clanged against metal. The fury in the Temple swept across the platform. In the midst of the rising bedlam, only Dr. Chesterly was calm. Holding Tim Donovan in his arms, he retreated from the storm.

Jimmy Christopher, as Z-7's call sounded, whipped about. Dr. Kalmar, defying the guns that stared at him, leaped from the dais. He plunged wildly into the throng pressing toward the entrance. He tore the crimson gown away; he plunged madly among the hundreds struggling out of the temple. Jimmy Christopher shouldered after him, fighting the power of the crowd. Desperately he fought his way through the arch to the companionway. He pushed upon a deck swarming with dismayed men and women. He worked along the rail seeking Dr. Kalmar in the turmoil.

A movement high in the colored air drew Jimmy Christopher's eyes. Dr. Kalmar had climbed a ladder to the superstructure of the deck. He was standing at the edge of a huge ventilator shaft. In both hands he was gripping small objects. He raised his hands as he peered down and saw Operator 5 plunging toward him. A fierce light glinted in his eyes; with a sudden motion he hurled the black cubes down into the shaft.

Deep in the ship, a terrific concussion sent flames leaping up the shaft. The vessel lurched and trembled in the sea. Through the screams of the hundreds now swarming on deck came the roaring sound of torrents pouring in through burst seams. Up through the ventilator funnels fumes gushed, followed by blinding fire. In the heart of the great ship, flames raged.

Operator 5 jerked himself up the ladder to the top of the superstructure; he fell to a crouch, peering at Dr. Kalmar silhouetted there against the rising flames. The doctor leaped forward. Operator 5 straightened with clenched fists. He drove out sharply as Dr. Kalmar's claws struck at his eyes. He slammed swift, powerful blows to the narrow, evil face. He jarred the doctor backward foot by foot. Kalmar recoiled in screaming fury—recoiled from the power of Jimmy Christopher's fists. He whirled—and a new shriek of terror burst from his lips. He fell sprawling past the edge of the shaft—plunged into the maw of the white-hot flames!

Operator 5 whirled away grimly. Over the heads of the terrorized throng he shouted: "Get down to the boats! Women first to the boats! Work fast!"

He leaped down to the deck. The companionways were clear now. Thickening fumes were flowing upward. Operator 5 fought his way through them back to the crimson temple. He saw Dr. Chesterly hurrying to the steps, carrying Clifford Morrell. He saw Z-7 following, bearing Tim Donovan. Jimmy Christopher stopped the chief; he took the boy in his arms.

"To the boats, Chief—quick! Tim!"

THE BOY peered vaguely into Operator 5's face. His lips trembled but he did not speak. Jimmy Christopher saw the Temple of the Crown filled with heightening flames; he hurried up the companionway. Striding along the rail, through gusting smoke, he saws boats clustering close. To their decks, women were hurrying. Men were mobbing at the heads of the accommodation ladders. Behind them, Intelligence men were enforcing orders....

Operator 5 waited while the passengers reached the smaller boats. Flames were streaming high into the air. The fire was spreading across the deck. The torrential roar of water mingled with the snarling of the blaze. A withering heat was carrying on the wind. The ship was listing heavily as the sea poured in.

Z-7 called frantically: "Down!" Operator 5 hurried down the steps while Intelligence men followed the chief. He struggled to the crowded deck of a Coast Guard cutter. Hugging Tim

Donovan close, he sank down as the boat cast off. The last man to leap to the rail called ringingly: "All off!"

The cutter swung away sharply. The sea, lighted by the flames, was bobbing with the small retreating craft. In the water, scores of men were swimming while the lightest boats circulated to pick them up. A white wake marked the course of the cutter as Operator 5 peered back at the torch in the sea....

A metallic scream came from the great vessel as it gave its last list. Its prow dipped. Its stern rose high and dripping from the water. Its flames quenched out as it dived downward, Turmoil spread through the sea as it vanished, leaving only a haze of smoke clinging to the surface.

The ship of the Golden Crown plunged the Master of Death to a doom that carried him beyond all possibility of resurrection....

CHAPTER 15
A CLASP OF HANDS

THE HOSPITAL room was hushed. Under spotless sheets, Tim Donovan lay against high pillows. Jimmy Christopher faced him. At the foot of the bed, Diane Elliot stood, her eyes glistening with tears; John Christopher watched solemnly. The Irish lad gazed at them uncertainly, as though through a bewildering fog.

"Tim," Jimmy Christopher said quietly. "You remember me, don't you, Tim? You remember us all?"

From the boy's lips the answer came slowly—an answer that

he had given again and again. "I don't remember. I don't remember you at all...."

Jimmy Christopher rose wretchedly. For hours he had been striving to reach beyond the blank wall of Tim Donovan's broken memory. He had brought the boy to the hospital at once; his joy at Tim's recovery was dimmed only by the fact that he and Diane and John Christopher had become total strangers.... His head wagged hopelessly as he turned to the corner table at the purr of a bell.

Z-7 spoke quickly over the wire. "We have completed our check on the disaster. As far as we can learn, none of those aboard the ship were lost except Dr. Kalmar and several of his lieutenants. Others of his men we are holding prisoners. I have already conferred with the President, and we shall take secret means of replacing the important office-holders whom Mr. Kalmar victimized. His organization is destroyed—his power it broken. The President wishes to see you to express his gratitude."

"Very well, Chief," Operator 5 answered solemnly. "I will come soon."

John Christopher spoke quietly as he turned away. "Son,—I realize now that you were right. I was half mad to insist that you leave Dr. Kalmar untouched. Seeing what he has done to Tim—"

Ex-Operator Q-6 broke off as a step sounded outside the door. Dr. Chesterly strode into the room. His gaze was bright as he whipped off his coat and hat and bent over Tim Donovan. He straightened to draw a small vial from his pocket—a vial filled with a golden liquid.

"This," he said, "is similar to the extract of Dr. Kalmar that I brought with me from the ship. I have analyzed it twice. I know all its ingredients. One of them is a hormone which Dr. Kalmar incorporated in order to affect the mind in a certain way. It brings about a condition of general amnesia—he afflicted the condition intentionally! I have prepared a new extract without that hormone."

Quickly, as Operator 5 watched, he filled a syringe with the fluid. "I have just come from Mr. Morrell's home. I made use of this preparation there. I scarcely dared hope it would be effective, but every indication shows that the boy's mental faculties are returning completely. It is possible—"

HE BENT above Tim Donovan. Carefully he drove the hypodermic needle home. He discharged the barrel and took the boy's wrist. Operator 5 leaned forward tensely, watching Tim Donovan's, face. Diane Elliot's hand clung to his warmly through a long period of silence. "Perhaps," Dr. Chesterly said quietly, "it is too much to hope that—"

He broke off. Jimmy Christopher went quickly to Tim Donovan's side. The boy was peering from face to face. A new light was shining in his eyes. His lips trembled. Suddenly he started up. He gazed into Operator 5's face. He blurted in a whisper:

"Jimmy! Jimmy!"

He rolled his head toward Operator 5.

Jimmy Christopher's aching throat tightened. A deep sigh broke from his lips—a sigh of profound relief and gratitude. He seized the hot hand of the little Irish lad. His voice rang vibrant with joy.

"Tim, old-timer! You remember! You remember now!"

THE SPIDER
- ❏ #1: The Spider Strikes — $13.95
- ❏ #2: The Wheel of Death — $13.95
- ❏ #3: Wings of the Black Death — $13.95
- ❏ #4: City of Flaming Shadows — $13.95
- ❏ #5: Empire of Doom! — $13.95
- ❏ #6: Citadel of Hell — $13.95
- ❏ #7: The Serpent of Destruction — $13.95
- ❏ #8: The Mad Horde — $13.95
- ❏ #9: Satan's Death Blast — $13.95
- ❏ #10: The Corpse Cargo — $13.95
- ❏ #11: Prince of the Red Looters — $13.95
- ❏ #12: Reign of the Silver Terror — $13.95
- ❏ #13: Builders of the Dark Empire — $13.95
- ❏ #14: Death's Crimson Juggernaut — $13.95
- ❏ #15: The Red Death Rain — $13.95
- ❏ #16: The City Destroyer — $13.95
- ❏ #17: The Pain Emperor — $13.95
- ❏ #18: The Flame Master — $13.95
- ❏ #19: Slaves of the Crime Master — $13.95
- ❏ #20: Reign of the Death Fiddler — $13.95
- ❏ #21: Hordes of the Red Butcher — $13.95
- ❏ #22: Dragon Lord of the Underworld — $13.95
- ❏ **NEW:** #23: Master of the Death-Madness — $13.95

THE MYSTERIOUS WU FANG
- ❏ #1: The Case of the Six Coffins — $12.95
- ❏ #2: The Case of the Scarlet Feather — $12.95
- ❏ #3: The Case of the Yellow Mask — $12.95
- ❏ #4: The Case of the Suicide Tomb — $12.95
- ❏ #5: The Case of the Green Death — $12.95
- ❏ #6: The Case of the Black Lotus — $12.95
- ❏ #7: The Case of the Hidden Scourge — $12.95

G-8 AND HIS BATTLE ACES
- ❏ #1: The Bat Staffel — $13.95

CAPTAIN SATAN
- ❏ #1: The Mask of the Damned — $13.95
- ❏ #2: Parole for the Dead — $13.95
- ❏ #3: The Dead Man Express — $13.95
- ❏ #4: A Ghost Rides the Dawn — $13.95
- ❏ #5: The Ambassador From Hell — $13.95

CAPTAIN ZERO
- ❏ #1: City of Deadly Sleep — $13.95
- ❏ #2: The Mark of Zero! — $13.95

OPERATOR 5
- ❏ #1: The Masked Invasion — $13.95
- ❏ #2: The Invisible Empire — $13.95
- ❏ #3: The Yellow Scourge — $13.95
- ❏ #4: The Melting Death — $13.95
- ❏ #5: Cavern of the Damned — $13.95
- ❏ #6: Master of Broken Men — $13.95
- ❏ #7: Invasion of the Dark Legions — $13.95
- ❏ #8: The Green Death Mists — $13.95
- ❏ #9: Legions of Starvation — $13.95
- ❏ #10: The Red Invader — $13.95
- ❏ #11: The League of War-Monsters — $13.95
- ❏ **NEW:** #12: The Army of the Dead — $13.95

DUSTY AYRES AND HIS BATTLE BIRDS
- ❏ #1: Black Lightning! — $13.95
- ❏ #2: Crimson Doom — $13.95
- ❏ #3: The Purple Tornado — $13.95
- ❏ #4: The Screaming Eye — $13.95
- ❏ #5: The Green Thunderbolt — $13.95
- ❏ #6: The Red Destroyer — $13.95
- ❏ #7: The White Death — $13.95
- ❏ #8: The Black Avenger — $13.95
- ❏ #9: The Silver Typhoon — $13.95
- ❏ #10: The Troposphere F-S — $13.95
- ❏ #11: The Blue Cyclone — $13.95
- ❏ #12: The Tesla Raiders — $13.95

DR. YEN SIN
- ❏ #1: Mystery of the Dragon's Shadow — $12.95
- ❏ #2: Mystery of the Golden Skull — $12.95
- ❏ #3: Mystery of the Singing Mummies — $12.95

MAVERICKS
- ❏ #1: Five Against the Law — $12.95
- ❏ #2: Mesquite Manhunters — $12.95
- ❏ #3: Bait for the Lobo Pack — $12.95
- ❏ #4: Doc Grimson's Outlaw Posse — $12.95
- ❏ #5: Charlie Parr's Gunsmoke Cure — $12.95